ANNE FINE

-Trilogy-

BILL'S NEW FROCK
THE COUNTRY PANCAKE
THE ANGEL OF NITSHILL ROAD

Illustrated by Philippe Dupasquier and Kate Aldous

MAMMOTH

First published in Great Britain as three separate volumes:

Bill's New Frock
First published 1989 by Methuen Children's Books Ltd
Published 1990 by Mammoth

The Country Pancake
First published 1989 by Methuen Children's Books Ltd
Published 1991 by Mammoth

The Angel of Nitshill Road
First published 1992 by Methuen Children's Books Ltd
Published 1993 by Mammoth

This omnibus edition first published 1994 by Mammoth
an imprint of Reed Consumer Books Ltd
Michelin House, 81 Fulham Road, London SW3 6RB
and Auckland, Melbourne, Singapore and Toronto

Reprinted 1994

ISBN 0 7497 1825 0

A CIP catalogue record for this title is available from the British Library

Printed and bound in Great Britain by Cox & Wyman Ltd, Reading, Berkshire

Contents

Bill's New Frock

· 1 ·

A Really Awful Start

When Bill Simpson woke up on Monday morning, he found he was a girl.

He was still standing staring at himself in the mirror, quite baffled, when his mother swept in.

'Why don't you wear this pretty pink dress?' she said.

'I *never* wear dresses,' Bill burst out.

'I know,' his mother said. 'It's such a pity.'

And, to his astonishment, before he could even begin to argue, she had dropped the dress over his head and zipped up the back.

'I'll leave you to do up the shell buttons,' she said. 'They're a bit fiddly and I'm late for work.'

And she swept out, leaving him staring in dismay at the mirror. In it, a girl with his curly red hair and wearing a pretty pink frock with fiddly shell buttons was staring back at him in equal dismay.

'This can't be true,' Bill Simpson said to himself. 'This cannot be true!'

He stepped out of his bedroom just as his father was rushing past. He, too, was late in getting off to work.

Mr Simpson leaned over and planted a kiss on Bill's cheek.

'Bye, Poppet,' he said, ruffling Bill's curls. 'You look very sweet today. It's not often we see you in a frock, is it?'

He ran down the stairs and out of the

house so quickly he didn't see Bill's scowl, or hear what he muttered savagely under his breath.

Bella the cat didn't seem to notice any difference. She purred and rubbed her soft, furry body around his ankles in exactly the same way as she always did.

And Bill found himself spooning up his cornflakes as usual. It was as if he couldn't help it. He left the house at the usual time, too. He didn't seem to have any choice. Things, though odd, were just going on in their own way, as in a dream.

Or it could be a nightmare! For hanging about on the corner was the gang of boys from the other school. Bill recognised the one they called Mean Malcolm in his purple studded jacket.

I think I'll go round the long way instead, Bill thought to himself. I don't want to be tripped up in one of their nasty scuffles, like last week, when all the scabs were kicked off my ankle.

Then Bill heard the most piercing whistle.

He looked around to see where the noise was coming from, then realised Mean Malcolm was whistling at him!

Bill Simpson blushed so pink that all his freckles disappeared. He felt so foolish he forgot to turn off at the next corner to go round the long way. He ended up walking right past the gang.

Mean Malcolm just sprawled against the railings, whistling at Bill as he went by wearing his pretty pink frock with shell buttons.

Bill Simpson thought to himself: I'd rather have the scabs kicked off my ankle!

When he reached the main road, there was an elderly woman with curly grey hair already standing at the kerb. To feel safe from the gang, he stood at her side.

'Give me your hand, little girl,' she said. 'I'll see us both safely across the road.'

'No, really,' insisted Bill. 'I'm fine, honestly. I cross here every day by myself.'

The woman simply didn't listen. She just

reached down and grasped his wrist, hauling him after her across the road.

On the far side, she looked down approvingly as she released him.

'That's such a pretty frock!' she said. 'You mind you keep it nice and clean.'

Rather than say something disagreeable, Bill ran off quickly.

The headmaster was standing at the school gates, holding his watch in the palm of his hand, watching the last few stragglers arrive.

'Get your skates on, Stephen Irwin!' he yelled. And: '*Move*, Tom Warren!'

Another boy charged round the corner and cut in front of Bill.

'Late, Andrew!' the headmaster called out fiercely. 'Late, late, late!'

Then it was Bill's turn to go past.

'That's right ' the headmaster called out encouragingly. 'Hurry along, dear. We don't want to miss assembly, do we?'

And he followed Bill up the path to the school.

Assembly always took place in the main hall. After the hymn, everyone was told to sit on the floor, as usual. Desperately, Bill tried to tuck the pretty pink dress in tightly around his bare legs.

Mrs Collins leaned forward on her canvas chair.

'Stop fidgeting with your frock, dear,' she told him. 'You're getting nasty, grubby fingerprints all round the hem.'

Bill glowered all through the rest of assembly. At the end, everybody stood up as usual.

'Now I need four strong volunteers to carry a table across to the nursery,' announced the headmaster. 'Who wants to go?'

Practically everybody in the hall raised a hand. Everyone liked a trip over the playground. In the nursery they had music and water and bright sloshy paints and tricycles and enormous lego. And if you kept your head down and didn't talk too much or too loudly, it might be a good few minutes before anyone realised you were really from one of the other classrooms, and shooed you back.

So the hall was a mass of waving hands.

The headmaster gazed around him.

Then he picked four boys.

On the way out of the hall, Bill Simpson heard Astrid complaining to Mrs Collins:

'It isn't fair! He *always* picks the boys to carry things.'

'Perhaps the table's quite heavy,' soothed Mrs Collins.

'None of the tables in this school are heavy,' said Astrid. 'And I know for a fact that I am stronger than at least two of the boys he picked.'

'It's true,' Bill said. 'Whenever we have a tug of war, everyone wants to have Astrid on their team.'

'Oh, well,' said Mrs Collins. 'It doesn't matter. No need to make such a fuss over nothing. It's only a silly old table.'

And when Astrid and Bill took up arguing again, she told them the subject was closed, rather sharply.

Back in the classroom, everyone settled down at their tables.

'We'll do our writing first, shall we?' said Mrs Collins. 'And after that, we'll reward ourselves with a story.'

While Mrs Collins handed out the writing books and everyone scrabbled for pencils and rubbers, Bill looked round his table.

He was the only one in a dress.

Flora was wearing trousers and a blue blouse. Kirsty and Nick were both wearing jeans and a shirt. Philip was wearing corduroy slacks and a red jumper, and Talilah wore bright red satin bloomers under her fancy silk top.

Yes, there was no doubt about it. Talilah looked snazzy enough to go dancing, but Bill was the only one in a frock.

Oh, this was awful! What on earth had happened? Why didn't anybody seem to have noticed? What could he do? When would it end?

Bill Simpson put his head in his hands, and covered his eyes.

'On with your work down there on table five,' warned Mrs Collins promptly.

She meant him. He knew it. So Bill picked up his pen and opened his books. He couldn't help it. He didn't seem to have any choice. Things were still going on in their own way, as in a dream.

He wrote more than he usually did. He wrote it more neatly than usual, too. If you looked back through the last few pages of his work, you'd see he'd done a really good job, for him.

But you wouldn't have thought so, the way Mrs Collins went on when she saw it.

'Look at this,' she scolded, stabbing her finger down on the page. 'This isn't very neat, is it? Look at this dirty smudge. And the edge of your book looks as if it's been *chewed!*'

She turned to Philip to inspect his book next. It was far messier than Bill's. It was more smudgy and more chewed-looking. The writing was untidy and irregular. Some of the letters were so enormous they looked

like giants herding the smaller letters haphazardly across the page.

'Not bad at all, Philip,' she said. 'Keep up the good work.'

Bill could scarcely believe his ears. He was outraged. As soon as she'd moved off, he reached out for Philip's book, laid it beside his own on the table, and compared the two.

'It isn't fair!' he complained bitterly. 'Your page is *much* worse than my page. She didn't say anything nice to *me*.'

Philip just shrugged and said:

'Well, girls are neater.'

Bill felt so cross he had to sit on his hands to stop himself from thumping Philip.

Up at her desk, Mrs Collins was leafing through the class reader: *Tales of Today and Yesterday*.

'Where are we?' she asked them. 'Where did we finish last week? Did we get to the end of *Polly the Pilot*?'

She turned the page.

'Ah!' she said. 'Here's a good old story you all know perfectly well, I'm sure. It's

Rapunzel. And today it's table five's turn to take the main parts.'

Looking up, she eyed all six of them sitting there waiting.

'You'll be the farmer,' she said to Nick. 'You be the farmer's wife,' to Talilah. 'Witch,' she said to Flora. 'Prince,' she said to Philip. 'Narrator,' she said to Kirsty.

Oh, no! Oh, no! Bill held his breath as Mrs Collins looked at him and said:

'The Lovely Rapunzel.'

Before Bill could protest, Talilah had started reading aloud. She and the farmer began with a furious argument about whether or not it was safe to steal a lettuce from the garden of the wicked witch next door, to feed their precious daughter Rapunzel. Once they'd got going, Bill didn't like to interrupt them, so he just sat and flicked over the pages, looking for his first speech.

It was a long wait. The Lovely Rapunzel didn't seem to *do* very much. She just got stolen out of spite by the Witch, and hidden away at the very top of a high stone tower which had no door. There she just sat quietly for about fifteen years, being no trouble and growing her hair.

She didn't try to escape. She didn't complain. She didn't even have any fights with the Witch.

So far as Bill Simpson could make out, she wasn't really worth rescuing. He wasn't at all sure why the Prince bothered. He certainly wouldn't have made the effort himself.

After three pages, there came a bit for Rapunzel.

'Oooooooooh!' Bill read out aloud. 'Oooooooooh!'

No, it wasn't much of a part. Or much of a life, come to that, if you thought about it.

Bill raised his hand. He couldn't help it.

'Yes?' Mrs Collins said. 'What's the problem?' She hated interruptions when they were reading.

'I don't see why Rapunzel just has to sit and wait for the Prince to come along and rescue her,' explained Bill. 'Why couldn't she plan her own escape? Why didn't she cut off all her lovely long hair herself, and braid it into a rope, and knot the rope to something, and then slide down it? Why did she have to just sit there and waste fifteen years waiting for a Prince?'

Mrs Collins narrowed her eyes at Bill Simpson.

'You're in a very funny mood today,' she

told him. 'Are you sure that you're feeling quite yourself?'

Was he feeling quite himself? In this frock? Bill stared around the room. Everyone's eyes were on him. They were all waiting to hear what he said. What could he say?

Mercifully, before he was forced to answer, the bell rang for playtime.

· 2 ·

The Wumpy Choo

Outside in the playground a few boys were already kicking a football about. Bill Simpson was just about to charge in and join them when he remembered what he was wearing. He'd look a bit daft if he took a tumble, he decided. Maybe just for once he'd try to think of something else to do during playtime.

Each boy who ran out of the school joined the football game on one side or another. What did the girls do? He looked around. Some perched along the nursery wall, chatting to one another. Others stood in the cloakroom porch, sharing secrets and giggling. There were a few more huddled in each corner of the playground. Each time the football came their way, one of them would give it a hefty boot back into the game. There were two girls trying to mark out a hopscotch frame; but every time the footballers ran over the lines they were drawing, the chalk was so badly scuffed that you couldn't see the squares any longer.

But it was rather chilly just standing about. The dress might be very pretty, but it was thin, and Bill's legs were bare. He decided to join the girls in the porch. At least they were out of the wind.

As he came up to them, Leila was saying: 'Martin bets no one dares kick a football straight through the cloakroom window!'

The girls all looked up at the cloakroom

window. So did Bill. As usual, the caretaker had pushed up the lower half of the window as far as it would go. It made quite a large square hole.

'*Anyone* could kick a football through there,' scoffed Kirsty.

'*I* could,' said Astrid.

'Easy,' agreed Leila.

'What do you get if you do it?' Bill asked them.

'A wumpy choo.'

'A wumpy choo?'

Bill Simpson was mystified.

'Yes,' Leila told him. 'A wumpy choo.'

Bill glanced round the little group of girls. Nobody else looked in the least bit baffled. Presumably they all knew about wumpy choos – whatever they were.

'I didn't know you could get wumpy choos round here,' said Flora.

So they were rare, were they? Like giant pandas.

'I'd *love* a wumpy choo,' said Sarah. 'But I'm not allowed because I'm allergic.'

Definitely an animal, then. A furry one. Bill's next door neighbour was allergic to furry animals, too.

'What colour is it?' asked Astrid. 'Is it a pink one?'

If it was still pink, thought Bill, it was probably a baby and hadn't grown a lot of fur.

'No,' Linda told them. 'I know exactly what colour it is because it's the very last one, and it's browny-yellow.'

Perhaps Martin hadn't been feeding it properly. Perhaps that was the reason its nice pink skin and fur had gone all browny-yellow.

Obviously it needed to be rescued – and fast!

He'd better take the bet.

'I'll do it,' he announced. 'I'll kick the football through the cloakroom window, and get the wumpy choo.'

Talilah gave him a bit of a look.

'You'd better be careful of your dress,' she warned. 'That football is filthy.'

'I'll manage,' said Bill Simpson. 'I know what I'm doing.'

The news, he noticed, spread like wildfire all along the line of girls perched on the nursery wall, and into the little huddles in the corners of the playground. All the girls turned to watch someone have a go at kicking a football straight through the cloakroom window.

'What's the bet?' they asked one another.

'A wumpy choo.'

Right then, thought Bill. No reason to hang about. It was a simple enough shot. All he needed was a football.

He walked towards the footballers in order to borrow theirs for a moment. Just as he did so, the game happened to swing his way and several boys charged past – knocking Bill flat on his back on the tarmac.

'Get out of the way!'

'*We're* playing here!'

Bill picked himself up. He was astonished. Usually if anyone walked into the football game, the players just thought they'd decided to join in. 'Come in on *our* side!' they'd yell. 'Be our goalie! Take over!'

This time it was as if they weren't so much playing football around him as *through* him.

'Get off the pitch!'

'Stop getting in our way! Go *round*!'

It was the frock again! He knew it!

'I want the ball,' yelled Bill to all the other players. 'I just want to borrow it for a minute – for a bet!'

Games always stopped for bets. It was a rule. But they all acted as if they hadn't even heard him.

'Out of our *way*!'

'You're spoiling the *game*!'

The ball happened to bounce Bill's way again, so he leaped up and caught it in his hands.

'I *need* it,' he explained. 'Just for a moment.'

The footballers gathered in a circle round him. They didn't look at all pleased at this interruption of the game. In fact, they

looked rather menacing, all standing there with narrowed eyes, scowling. If this was the sort of reception the girls had come to expect, no wonder they didn't stray far from the railings. No wonder they didn't ask to play.

'Give the ball back,' Rohan was really glowering now.

'Yes,' Martin agreed. 'Why can't you stay in your own bit of the playground?'

Mystified, Bill asked Martin:

'What bit?'

'The girls' bit, of course.'

Bill looked around. Girls were still perched along the nursery wall. Girls were still huddled in the porch. Girls still stood in tight little groups in each corner. No girl was more than a few feet into the playground itself. Even the pair who had been trying to mark out the hopscotch game had given up and gone away.

'Where's that, then?' asked Bill. 'Where's the girls' bit? Where *are* the girls supposed to play?'

'*I* don't know,' Martin answered irritably. '*Anywhere*. Just somewhere we're not already playing football.'

'But you're playing football all over *every single inch* of the playground!'

Martin glanced up at the clock on the church tower next door to the school. There were only two minutes left before the bell rang, and his team was down by one tiny goal.

He spread his hands in desperation.

'*Please* give the ball back,' he pleaded. 'What's it worth?'

For the life of him Bill Simpson couldn't understand why, if Martin wanted the ball back so badly, he couldn't just step forward and try to prise it away from his chest. Then he realised that Martin simply didn't dare. The two of them might end up in a bit of a shoving match, and then a real fight – and *no one* fights a girl in a pretty pink frock with fiddly shell buttons.

So he said cunningly:

'I'll tell you what it's worth. It's worth your very last wumpy choo!'

To his astonishment, Martin looked delighted.

'Done!' he said at once, and began digging deep in his trouser pocket.

He handed a tiny, wrappered rectangle over to Bill.

'There you are,' he said. 'Here it is. Now give me the football and get off the pitch!'

Bill Simpson looked down.

'What's this?' he asked.

'It's what you wanted,' Martin said. 'My very last 1p Chew.'

In silence, Bill Simpson handed over the football. Where he'd been clutching it tightly against his chest, there was now an enormous brown smudge.

In silence, Bill Simpson turned and walked away. If all the girls had not been standing around the edges of the playground watching him, he would have cried.

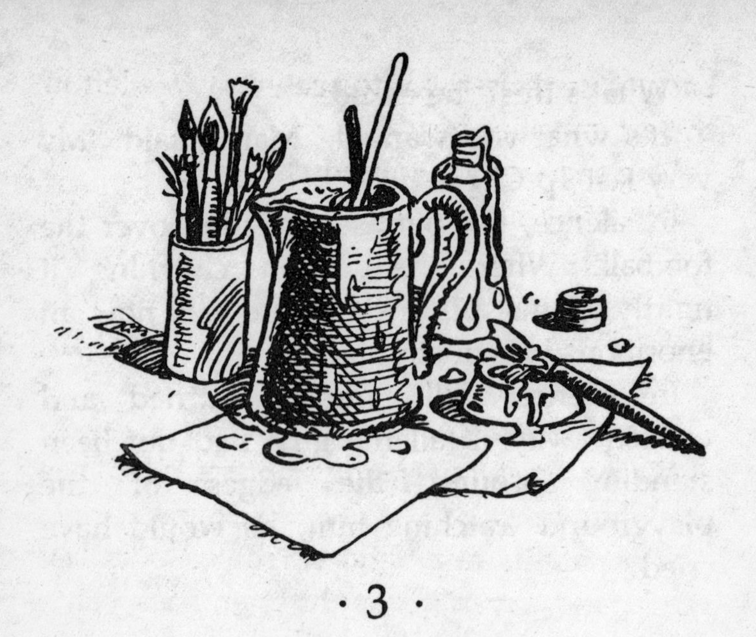

· 3 ·

Pink, Pink, Nothing But Pink

After break, it was art. Everyone helped to unfold the large, crackling plastic sheets and lay them over the table tops, and spread old newspapers over them. Then Mrs Collins sent Leila into the dark cupboard at the back of the classroom to see what was left in the art supplies box.

'Are there any coloured chalks left?'

'No, they're all gone.'

'Pastels, then.'

'They're still too damp to use after the roof leak.'

'What about clay?'

'It's all dried up.'

'There *must* be crayons. *Every* class has crayons.'

'The infants came and borrowed ours last week, and haven't brought them back yet.'

'Right, then. It will just have to be paint, as usual.'

So Leila dragged the heavy cardboard box full of paint tubs out of the cupboard, and everyone crowded round to choose their colours.

'Here's a pink.'

'What's that?'

'Pink.'

'More pink.'

'Pink.'

'I've found some blue – no, I haven't. It's empty.'

'I thought I'd found some green, but it's dried up.'

'There's no white. There's never any white. We haven't had white for years and years.'

'There's some pink here.'

'And this one's pink.'

'Pink, pink, nothing but pink!'

Everyone stood up, disappointed. Kirsty voiced everyone's disgust:

'What can you do with pink?' she demanded. 'You can't paint pink dogs or pink space vehicles or pink trees or pink battlefields, can you? If you can only find one colour, it's difficult enough. But if you've only got pink, it's practically *impossible*. What is there in the world that's all pink?'

'Yes. What's all pink?'

Everyone gazed around the room, looking for something that was all pink so they could paint it. Some of them stared at the pictures and posters pinned on the classroom walls. Others gazed out of the window, across the playground to the street and the shops. One or two of them glanced at one another –

And Kirsty looked at Bill.

'No!' Bill said. 'No, no, no! Not me! Absolutely not! You can't!'

Now everyone turned to look at Bill.

'No!' Bill insisted. 'I am *not all pink*!'

Now even Mrs Collins was looking at Bill.

'Pink frock,' she admitted slowly. 'And fiery hair. Rich rosy freckles and a nice deep blush. Yes, you'll do beautifully, dear. You're all pink.'

'I am *not pink*.'

But he was getting pinker by the minute. And by the time everyone had wandered back to their seats clutching their little plastic tubs of paint, you wouldn't have needed any other colour to do a really fine portrait of him.

'Perfect!' said Mrs Collins.

And taking Bill Simpson firmly by the hand, she tried to lead him over towards a chair in the middle of the room, where everyone would be able to see him clearly while they were painting him.

Bill tried to pull back. Mrs Collins turned in astonishment at his unwillingness, and let go of his hand quite suddenly. Bill staggered back – straight into Nicky who had just prised the top off his paint tub.

A huge glob of pink paint flew up in the air, and landed on Bill Simpson's frock. As everyone watched, it gathered itself, all fat and heavy at the bottom. Then, slowly, it slithered down between the folds of material, leaving a thick pink slug trail.

Bill Simpson watched in silence as a small pool of pink paint appeared on the floor, beside his left foot.

Grubby fingerprints round the hem; a huge muddy smudge on the front; a great slimy paint smear down the side. What next?

Mrs Collins inspected the damage, and shrugged.

'Well, never mind,' she said. 'It's only poster paint. I'm sure the frock will wash out beautifully.'

And, once again, she took his hand.

There was no fight left in Bill Simpson. Meekly, he allowed himself to be led to the middle of the room.

Mrs Collins arranged him neatly and comfortably on the little wooden chair.

'There,' she said triumphantly, placing a cherry-coloured exercise book in one of his hands as a last touch. 'All pink!'

She stepped back to admire her handiwork.

'Perfect!' she said again. 'Now is everyone happy?'

Bill Simpson could have tried to say something then, but he didn't bother. He reckoned there was no point. He knew that, whatever he said and whatever he did, this awful day would just keep sailing on in its own way, as in a dream. A curse was on him. A pink curse. He was, of all things, haunted by a pretty pink frock with fiddly shell buttons. He might as well give up struggling. Like poor Rapunzel trapped in her high stone tower, he'd just sit quietly, waiting to see what happened, hoping for rescue.

Meanwhile, the rest of the class had begun to complain.

'If we've only got pink to paint with, how are we supposed to do that great big

football-shaped smudge on the front of the frock? It's *brown*!'

'I can't paint all those grubby little fingerprints right round the hem of the dress, because they're *grey*.'

'Those shell buttons are a bit fiddly to paint!'

'I've done far too many freckles. What shall I do?'

'Wait till they're dry, then chip some off!'

Bill ignored everyone. He just sat there, waiting for time to go by. Even a bad dream couldn't last forever. His torment had to end some time, surely.

After half an hour or so, Mrs Collins came by, carrying a fresh jar of water over to table two.

'Do try not to look quite so *gloomy*, dear,' she murmured in Bill's ear as she walked past. 'You're spoiling people's paintings.'

And Bill was too miserable and defeated even to bother to scowl at the back of her head as she moved off.

· 4 ·

No Pockets

Perhaps Mrs Collins noticed how fed up he looked. Perhaps she was grateful to him for sitting so still for so long, and being so pink. Or maybe it was just Bill's eye she happened to catch first. But, whatever the reason, it was Bill Simpson she chose to take her spare key back to the office.

'That's helpful of you,' she said, pressing the key into his hand. 'Just give it to Mrs Band-araina. She's expecting it. And hurry back.'

Everyone else looked up from their maths books and watched enviously as he left the classroom and shut the door firmly behind him.

Outside, in the deserted corridor, one thought and one thought only was in Bill Simpson's mind: lavatories! Silently he crept along. Should he turn left, into the BOYS, and risk hoots and catcalls of astonishment if anyone caught him there in his pretty pink frock? Or should he turn right, into the GIRLS, where for a boy even to be found hanging around the doorway was to risk terrible trouble?

Girls' lavatories were more *private*. At least he could struggle with the frock in peace . . .

Bill made his choice. Peering back over his shoulder like some spy from an old black and white film, he scuttled hastily into the GIRLS.

When, two minutes later, he stuck his head back out through the swing doors, the corridor was still empty. Sighing with relief, Bill stepped out. He took his time now, dawdling along towards the school office, swinging the key from his fingers and stopping to peer at each painting on the wall. After his heart-stopping rush in and out of the

girls' lavatories, Bill reckoned that he'd earned a break.

But just as he turned the corner, who should he see backing out of a cupboard but the headmaster!

Bill Simpson started looking sharp. Lifting his chin, he walked a lot faster. He was almost safely past the headmaster when he was stopped.

A hand fell on the top of his head.

'You look very sensible and responsible,' the headmaster said. 'Not dawdling along, peering at all the paintings, taking your time. Are you going to the office on an errand for your teacher? Would you do me a favour and take these coloured inks to Mrs Bandaraina?'

And he held out a handful of tiny glass bottles.

Bill put out his free hand, and the headmaster tipped the tiny glass bottles onto his outstretched palm.

'Whatever you do, don't drop them,' he warned. And then he dived back in his cupboard.

Bill went on. He'd hardly reached the short flight of stairs when the school nurse came up them the other way, carrying a pile of yellow forms in her arms, and walking faster than most people run.

'Ah!' she said, spotting Bill. 'Just what I need! Someone who can take these medical forms to the office for me, so I can rush straight across to the nursery before the bell rings.'

She didn't exactly ask. And she didn't exactly wait to see if Bill minded. She just thrust the stack of yellow medical forms into his arms, and hurried off.

'And they're in perfect, alphabetical order,' she called back over her shoulder. 'So, whatever you do, don't drop them!'

Problem, thought Bill. One false move, and everything would fall to the floor – spare key, little glass ink bottles, medical forms in perfect, alphabetical order – the lot.

The key and the coloured inks would just have to go in his pockets.

Pockets?

Carefully, Bill squatted in the corridor and

lowered the pile of yellow medical forms to the floor, taking care that he didn't lose the key or drop the little glass bottles of coloured ink.

Then he felt all round the pretty pink frock for a pocket. He pushed and shoved at rather frilly places here and there, wherever he thought one might be hidden. But though he heard the material rip once or twice, and felt his hands go through the holes he'd accidentally torn, there were no pockets there.

No. Not one pocket. Yards and yards of material. Pleats, frills, bows, scallops, fancy loops. But not one pocket. Whoever designed the dress had gone to all the trouble of matching the imitation lace round the hem with the imitation lace round the collar, and fitting a zip in so neatly that it was practically invisible, and putting comfortable elastic around the little puffy sleeves.

But they just hadn't bothered to put in a pocket.

Bill was *amazed*. How was a person in a frock like this supposed to *survive*? How were they expected to get along without any pockets? It can't have been the only dress of its kind that was made. Other people must wear them. Where did they put their money, for heaven's sake? Did they keep it, all damp and hot and sticky, in the palms of their hands all day? Where did they put the sweets their friends gave them if they wanted to save them for later? What did they do if someone returned their pencil sharpener to them outside in break?

How can you *live* without pockets? How can you? How *can* you?

Bill put his head in his hands, and groaned.

Then he tried to pull himself together. This couldn't last forever. This couldn't go on. No boy could turn into a girl and stay that way without anyone – even his mother and teacher and schoolfriends – noticing any real difference. It must be a bad dream. It *felt* like a nightmare . . .

He'd just keep calm and steady and wait till the horror of it all was over. He'd just get on with the job in hand.

And the job in hand was to get all these things safely to the school office.

Bill gathered up the yellow medical forms. On top of them he put the coloured inks, right in the middle so they would not roll over the edge and smash on the floor. He wedged the key between the inks so it would not slide off the side. Then, very carefully, he started down the corridor again, towards the office.

Before he'd gone a dozen steps, he heard a rapping on the nearest window.

He turned to look. It was the caretaker.

The caretaker leaned through the window.

'Off to the office, are you?' he asked. 'Do us a favour. Take these tennis balls with you. Ask Mrs Bandaraina to lock them away.'

And before Bill could argue, the caretaker tipped seven tennis balls onto the carefully stacked pile in Bill's arms.

Bill stood for a moment, steadying his load. He let the medical forms dip a bit in the middle to make a sort of hollow to keep the balls together and stop them rolling off over every side. Then, even more carefully than before – step by tiny, gentle step – he made for the office again.

When he was only a few yards away he saw Mrs Bandaraina lift her head from her typing and glance through the open doorway and notice him, shuffling, barely an inch at a time, towards her.

Each step seemed to take forever. Everything in his pile seemed to be wobbling dangerously. Everything in his pile seemed to be sliding closer to the edge.

'My!' Mrs Bandaraina said, watching his snail-slow progress. 'Aren't you the careful one, taking such care not to spill coloured ink on your sweet little frock!'

It wasn't Bill's fault. It was because she said 'sweet little frock!'. A shudder of pure fury rose through his body and made his hands shake. He didn't know the yellow forms were going to slip from his grasp and slither out of alphabetical order across the floor. He didn't know the little glass bottles would fall and smash. He didn't know the seven tennis balls would bounce up and down in the bright coloured pools of spilt inks. He didn't know the spare key would end up submerged in a puddle of purple.

Bill Simpson tried very hard not to narrow his eyes at Mrs Bandaraina and blame her for everything as she slid off her office chair to help him. He tried very hard to look grateful as she swept a handful of tissues out of the box on her desk and helped him mop and wipe, and gather rainbow- spotted tennis balls. And he tried to look pleasant while she tipped the slivers of shattered glass in the waste basket, and helped him shuffle all the medical forms back into alphabetical order.

But once back in the corridor again, and alone, he couldn't help muttering something quite rude, and quite loudly, about the sort of person who would design a pretty pink frock with no pockets, and expect other people to go around wearing it.

· 5 ·

The Big Fight

It rained all through the lunch hour. The sky went grey, the windows misted over, and from overhead came the steady gunfire sound of huge raindrops pinging smartly on the skylight.

And Mrs Collins slipped into one of her dark wet-break moods.

Everyone knew the signs: the eyebrows knitting together over her nose; the lines across her forehead deepening to furrows; her lips thinning into tightened purse strings.

Everyone knew it was not the time to cause trouble.

So as the rain beat heavily against the window panes, everyone crept quietly around the classroom, trying to look as if they were up to something useful or sensible, or, at the very least, quiet.

And out of the storeroom came the old comic box.

Nobody *meant* to make a great noise and a fuss. All anyone wanted was simply to go to the box, dip in their hand, and pick out a couple of comics they liked. Nobody *meant* to end up in a scrum, pushing and shoving the others out of the way, using their elbows, desperate to get an arm in and whip out a favourite comic before someone else leaned over and snatched it.

Nobody *meant* to end up in a riot.

'SILENCE!' roared Mrs Collins. 'Go back to

your places at once! I will give out the comics *myself*.'

As she came over, everyone melted away from the comic box and drifted back to their own favourite wet-break places. Talilah and Kirsty sat side by side on the fat radiator pipes. Flora perched on the window sill. Philip and Nicky sprawled on the floor beneath table five, and Bill, who probably would have joined them on any other wet day, glanced down at all the marks and smears and tears he already had on his pretty pink frock, and then at the muddy grime and footprints all over the floor where his friends were – and thought better of it.

He settled himself alone, leaning his chair back against the wall, and waited for Mrs Collins to hand round the comics.

They were a shabby and a dog-eared lot. It was with a slight shudder of disgust that Mrs Collins dipped her arms in the box to lift them out, and started round the room. Like everyone else, Bill hoped so hard that she would go round his way first, but he was out of luck.

She went the other way. It took her ages.

All of the Beanos went first, of course. Then all the Dandies. She gave out a Hotspur and a Lion, then several Bunties and some Victors.

By the time she reached Bill Simpson, there was very little left.

'Mandy?' she offered him. 'Or would you prefer a June or a Judy?'

He could tell from the look on her face that she wasn't in the mood for discussion. So he contented himself with replying coldly:

'I'll have a Thunder, please. Or a Hornet.'

'No more Hornets,' she said, leafing through the last three or four comics left in her hand. 'No Thunders, either. I thought I might still have a Valiant, but I must have given that to Rohan.'

She thrust a Bunty towards him.

'There you are,' she said. 'You'll enjoy this. There's almost no pages missing at all.'

And off she went, back to her desk.

Bill glanced down at the comic in his hands. He didn't care for the look of it at all. He didn't want to read it. What use was a Bunty?

He wanted a Beano or a Dandy or a Thunder, and that was that.

Melissa was sitting only a few feet away, absorbed in a Beano.

Bill leaned across.

'Hey, Melissa,' he called softly. 'Here's a Bunty with all the pages and no torn bits. Do you want to swap?'

Melissa gazed at him over her comic, her eyes widening even more as she realized he was serious.

'You must be *joking,*' she said, and went back to her Beano.

Bill tried the other side.

Flora was sitting firmly on one Dandy, and reading another.

'Flora,' called Bill. 'Would you like a Bunty?'

'No, thank you,' Flora said politely, without so much as raising her eyes from the page.

Bill Simpson decided to have a go at one of the boys.

'Rohan!' he hissed. 'Hey! Rohan! I'll swap you my practically brand new comic here for

your tatty old Valiant with hardly any pages left.'

'What's your comic?' asked Rohan. 'Is it a Hotspur?'

'No,' Bill confessed. 'No. It's a Bunty.'

Rohan just sniggered and went back to his comic. Clearly he thought it was just a good joke.

Bill tried one last time.

'Martin,' he offered. 'Will you swap with me as soon as you've finished that Victor?'

Martin said:

'Sure. What have you got there?'

Bill said as softly as he could:

'Bunty.'

'What?' Martin said. *'What?'*

So Bill Simpson had to tell him all over again.

Martin snorted.

'No thanks,' he said. 'No *thanks*. I'll swap mine with Melissa's Beano instead.'

And he went back to his reading.

Bill blamed Mrs Collins, frankly. Though he couldn't prove it, and wouldn't dare ask, he firmly suspected that, if he had not been wearing the pretty pink frock, he would never have ended up with the Bunty. Mrs Collins could easily have arranged things some other way. She might have ordered Flora to give him the Dandy she was sitting on, to keep him going. Or she might have suggested to Rohan that Bill and he sit close together to read the Valiant at the same time.

He couldn't prove it – no, he couldn't prove it. But he felt sore about it all the same.

But clearly there was nothing to be done now. It was too late. Everyone else was reading quietly, and Mrs Collins didn't look as if she would take at all kindly to any complaints. He could either waste the whole lunch break trying, completely in vain, to find someone who would trade their comic for his Bunty, or he could give up and just read the Bunty.

He read the Bunty.

And it wasn't that bad. He read the story about the sneaky schoolteacher who switched the examination papers around so that her own spoilt and lazy daughter would win the one and only college place. He read the story about the brave orphan gypsy girl who led her lame pony carefully at night through a dangerous war zone. He was still quite absorbed in the very funny tale of three girls who had somehow found themselves responsible for an enormous hippopotamus with an even more enormous appetite, when a shadow fell over the page.

Flora was holding out a Dandy.

'Swap?'

'In a minute. Let me finish this.'

'Now or never,' said Flora.

'All right, then,' said Bill.

A little regretfully – he wouldn't have minded finding out what the hippo ate next – Bill handed over his Bunty and took the Dandy. No sooner had he turned the first page than yet another shadow fell on him, and Rohan was standing at his side.

'Here. You take this, and I'll have that one.'

In his hand, Rohan held a copy of June.

'No, thanks,' said Bill, and he went back to his reading.

'Come on,' said Rohan. 'Don't be mean. Swap comics with me. I don't want this one.'

'I don't want it either.'

'You haven't read it.'

'I am reading *this*.'

And Bill shook his Dandy in Rohan's face.

That was his first big mistake. His second big mistake was not moving fast enough when Rohan reached out and tried to snatch it.

Rohan's grip tightened over the top of the comic.

'Let go of my Dandy!'

'Don't be so *mean*!'

'*Mean*? Why *should* I give you my Dandy and take your rotten June?'

'Because you might *like* it,' said Rohan. 'And I definitely *won't*.'

The penny dropped. It was the frock again. Bill couldn't believe it. Hadn't the morning been agonising enough? Now was even his lunch break going to be ruined because he just happened to be wearing this stupid, silly curse of a dress? If this was the sort of thing that kept happening to you if you came to school in a frilly pink frock, no wonder all the girls wore jeans!

Bill Simpson had had quite enough.

'Let go of my comic,' he warned Rohan in a soft and dangerous voice. 'Let go of it or I shall mash you.'

In answer to this threat, Rohan tugged harder.

The Dandy began to tear.

'Let go!' repeated Bill Simpson.

Rohan pulled harder. Bill Simpson hit him. He clenched his fist and punched Rohan on the shoulder as hard as he could.

Rohan yelped in pain, and dropped his half of the comic.

Though his heart was thumping so fiercely

his eyes couldn't settle on the pictures, let alone read the print, Bill Simpson pretended he had calmly gone back to his Dandy.

Until Rohan kicked out at him.

In fact, his foot didn't touch Bill at all. It tangled instead in the folds of the pretty pink dress. But it did leave a great, black criss-cross footprint on the flimsy material, and it was a kick.

And Bill was furious. He leaped to his feet and started hitting Rohan as hard as he could. Rohan put up his own fists to defend himself. And, within seconds, they were having a fight.

The noise was tremendous. Everyone in the classroom started up at once – some asking who had started the fight, some egging on one side or another, some telling both of them to stop.

Then, as the blows rained down on either side, everyone around fell silent. For this was the first really big fight ever seen in the classroom itself, and it was shocking. No one was ever surprised to see the odd, sly kick on someone's ankle. Everyone had noticed the occasional deliberate tripping up, or hard nudge.

But nothing like this. Not a real big fight. Never.

It was Mrs Collins who put a stop to it. Striding across the room in a fury, she grasped both of them by the shoulder and hauled them apart.

Both were scarlet with rage.

'How *dare* you?' shouted Mrs Collins. 'How DARE you?'

She was enraged, too. No one had ever seen her looking so angry. Her dark wet-break mood had turned so fierce she looked fit to kill. Her eyes were flashing, her nose gone pointy, and her mouth shrunk to a lemon-sucking sliver.

'How *dare* you!'

Rohan and Bill stood glowering at one another.

'What *is* going on? Who *started* this fight?'

'It wasn't *my* fault,' snarled Rohan. '*I* didn't start it.'

'You *did*,' snarled Bill, clenching his fists again. 'You *kicked* me!'

He showed the footprint on his pretty pink frock.

'You punched me first,' insisted Rohan, rubbing his shoulder hard to try to get sympathy from the bystanders.

But Mrs Collins, for one, wasn't impressed. She didn't even appear to have heard what he said. She was busy leaning over to look at the footprint on Bill Simpson's frock.

'This is shocking, Rohan,' she said. 'Shocking! To leave a footprint as clear as this on the frock, you must have lashed out really hard with your foot.'

'I was punched first!'

But Rohan's wailing did him no good. A look of scorn came over Mrs Collin's face. Though she said nothing out loud, you could almost hear her thinking: *How could a little thump on the shoulder from someone in a pretty pink frock excuse a great big kick from someone wearing heavy Doc Marten boots?*

So, thought Bill Simpson quietly to himself.

There can be *one* advantage to wearing a frock.

It didn't last for long, though. She punished them both. She put them at neighbouring desks, and made them write *Fighting is stupid and fighting is ugly* in their best handwriting over and over again, till the bell rang.

They sat with exactly the same sour look on their faces. Both were still furious at the unfairness of it all. To everyone else, they looked for all the world like a pair of scowling and bad-tempered twins.

And every now and again, someone would tiptoe past and whisper in Rohan's ear:

'You look so *angry*.'

But in Bill's they whispered:

'You look so *upset*.'

· 6 ·

Letting Paul Win

As soon as the bell rang for the end of the lunch break, the sun began to shine again. It sailed out from silvery edges of cloud, and blazed over the playground.

The puddles on the tarmac steamed gently, and then disappeared. The damp stains on the nursery wall dried. Sunlight reflected brightly off the rooftops.

Mrs Collins stared out of the window, shaking her head in quiet disbelief. Then she turned to the class.

'Pack up your work,' she said. 'I don't care if lunch break is over. We're going outside before it starts raining all over again.'

The class was astonished. It wasn't often Mrs Collins ignored the timetable on the back of the door. It was hard enough to get her to let them take time off to make decorations at Christmas, or paint the back-cloth if they did a little play. Now here she was offering an hour or so in the sunshine without being asked.

Nobody argued. They slid their books into neat piles, and put their pens and pencils and rubbers away.

'Races!' said Mrs Collins. 'We'll have a few races. We haven't had races for *such* a long time.'

They spilled down the steps out into the playground, and Mrs Collins led them quietly round to the back of the nursery where there was grass. Races were pleasanter on grass, and this patch was not even overlooked by classes still imprisoned in front of their work books.

Out here they could have a really good time.

The races came in every size and description, one after another, as fast as Mrs Collins could think them up. The light haired raced against the dark haired. The straight haired raced against the curly haired.

'Those in frocks against those in trousers!' roared Mrs Collins.

She looked round. Only Bill had a frock on.

'Forget it!' called Mrs Collins. 'That race is cancelled. Think of something else!'

Someone did. Those wearing red raced against those wearing no red at all. Those who liked cats better than dogs raced against those who preferred dogs to cats. The first five in the class (in alphabetical order) raced against the next five, and so on and so on.

The first few times he ran, Bill slowed himself up, trying to keep down the flapping sides of his dress. Then he stopped bothering. If he were in shorts, he wouldn't mind, he decided. So why risk losing a good race just because he was haunted by a silly pink frock. He might be right back to normal tomorrow – but you could just bet there wouldn't be races again!

Soon everyone, not just Bill, felt much better. Their bodies unstiffened, their heads felt clearer, their spirits rose. Even Paul, who had a serious illness when he was a baby and could hardly run, scampered about, enjoying coming in last in the races.

Mrs Collins had cheered up enormously, too.

'Those who have real tin dustbins against those whose families put rubbish out in large, plastic bags!'

Everyone has rubbish. So everyone stood in line.

'There's far too many again,' said Mrs Collins. 'We shall have to have heats.'

As usual she divided them in fives, with one left over. This time it was Paul, so she sent him off in a heat of his own. He pranced along in his curious, loping fashion, and threw himself merrily over the finishing line.

'I'm in the finals now! I won my heat!'

Mrs Collins pushed the hair back from her face. She was hot.

'Small break before this final,' she called. 'All of you stay here quietly while I slip inside for a moment. *Whispering only!*'

And she hurried off to fetch a quick drink.

Bill tucked the pink frock in tightly around his legs and lay back. The grass felt tickly under his arms and his neck. Above, the fat clouds sailed over an enormous sky. The cool breeze fanned his face. He felt perfectly happy.

He heard Astrid whispering in his ear:

'You're in this final, aren't you? You won your heat. So did I. So did Talilah and Kirsty.'

'And Paul,' Bill reminded Astrid. 'He won his heat, too.'

He narrowed his eyes against the sunlight to make them water and form rainbows between his eyelashes.

'Kirsty will win,' said Astrid. 'She's the best runner in the whole class. And I only won my heat because Nicky tripped.'

'Races aren't nearly so much fun,' said

Talilah, 'when you know exactly who's going to win.'

'It must be much worse,' whispered Kirsty, 'if you're someone like Paul, and know you're going to lose.'

'Paul can't have won a race in his whole life!'

Bill blinked the rainbows away. Now he was seeing shapes in clouds – a pig, a jug, a serpent with three heads, a wigwam.

Beside him, the girls were in one of their huddles, still whispering away.

'What if Paul *did* win, though?'

'He'd be so *thrilled*.'

'Wouldn't his Mum be pleased? She's so nice. She sees me over Blackheath Road every morning.'

'She'd think we'd fixed it so her Paul won, though. *And* so would Paul.'

'Not if we were clever.'

'Not if we thought it out first, and made it look *good*.'

Bill barely listened. He was distracted by the clouds still. He watched his three-headed serpent float over the wide sky overhead, and turn, slowly, slowly, into a giant wheelbarrow.

The whispering at his side went on and on.

Then:

'Right,' Kirsty said. 'That's *settled*.'

She turned to Bill.

'Now don't *forget*,' she whispered sternly. 'Just as you're reaching the line, you get a really bad attack of stitch. You can't go on. You let Paul go past you. You let Paul win, is that understood?'

Bill took a last look at his cloud wheelbarrow. One of its handles was just floating away.

'Right-ho,' he agreed. It wasn't exactly his idea of a really good race – letting Paul win. But that was girls for you, wasn't it? Put them in a group and *order* them to whisper, and they'd be bound to come up with something like this.

And what did it matter on such a lovely afternoon? If it would make Paul happy, let him win the race.

'On your marks!'

Mrs Collins strode round the corner. They jumped to their feet. Astrid looked horrified.

'The back of your dress is *covered* with grass stains!' she said to Bill. '*And* they're the sort that never come out!'

Bill shrugged, and made for the starting line. Paul was already there, hopping about with excitement. Astrid, Talilah and Kirsty took their places.

'Get set!'

Kirsty turned to Bill.

'Bad luck, then,' she whispered, and grinned.

Bill winked back.

'Go!'

Talilah, Kirsty and Bill set off running. Paul shot away from the line in one of his extraordinary leaps. And as soon as he was a few feet ahead of Astrid, she fell tidily sideways and rolled on the ground, clutching her foot.

'Oh, my ankle!' she groaned – but softly, so that Paul would not overhear her, and turn back to help. 'My ankle's gone all wobbly. I can't run at all.'

Then, cheerfully, she picked herself up and, limping heavily on the wrong foot, returned to the others waiting around the line.

'Bad luck!'

'Never mind, Astrid!'

Up at the front of the race, Kirsty and Talilah seemed to be battling it out for first place. Now Kirsty had the edge, now Talilah. Then Kirsty was in front again. But just as she might have pulled ahead of Talilah, the two girls' bodies seemed to become entangled: ankles wrapped round ankles, legs wrapped round legs.

Together they fell, rolling over and over on the grass, giggling loudly.

As Bill ran up, they managed somehow to roll in his way and bring him to a standstill. Twice he tried to get round them, but they rolled the way he was going. Paul was catching up behind, so finally Bill just jumped over their wildly flailing arms and legs. As he did so, he saw Kirsty wink.

Of course! He'd almost forgotten! Let Paul win!

And now there were only himself and Paul left in the race. And so he would have to fall back and let him pull ahead very soon. The winning line was not all that far away. He was already halfway round the circuit.

Right then.

Bill tried to slow his pace. He couldn't do it. It was remarkable, but though he could pound along like a well-oiled machine, and leap over tufts of rough grass without thinking, and even do a fancy sideways hop when he saw something glinting like broken glass beneath his foot, he couldn't slow down. He just couldn't do it.

He couldn't let Paul win.

And it wasn't as if who won the race was important. He knew that. A race might start with those who walked to school running against those who came on a bus or by car, but by the time someone had won, no one could even remember what the race was about.

So it wasn't important.

But still he couldn't slow up and let Paul win. It would look quite ridiculous, he thought. Everyone would guess, and Paul would be really embarrassed.

And then he remembered that he wasn't *supposed* to slow down. The girls had sat in their huddle and worked all this out before the race began. They'd *known* he wouldn't be able to slow down. They'd thought it all out – weren't girls *amazing*?

He was supposed to pretend to have a stitch.

Right, then.

But he couldn't do that, either! And time was running out so fast. He'd almost completed the circuit. There was the finishing line, looming up only a few metres ahead. And there was the whole class, watching.

And he could not stop and double over, grimacing and clutching his stomach as though in the grip of a fierce spasm of pain, pretending he had a stitch.

It wasn't that he couldn't act. It wasn't that he would feel embarrassed about it. It was simply that he could not bring himself to do it. There was the finishing line, and here was he, and there was Paul a really long way behind him now. He wanted to reach the line first, that was all. He didn't want to let Paul win.

He wanted to win *himself*.

Ten metres to go. Now or never. The girls would *kill* him if he let them down.

Five metres. Now or never. Surely even the girls, if they had come this far, would find it difficult to stop and lose.

Three metres. Now or never.

One metre. Now.

There! Over the line!

(Never).

A smile of triumph spread across his face. He'd won. He'd *won!*

He shut his eyes, the better to appreciate the sound of hands clapping, and the cheers.

Then, opening them, he met a cold,

hostile glare from Astrid. And one from Kirsty. And one from Talilah.

There was everybody else, cheering and applauding madly. And there were three pairs of witch eyes, glowering at him balefully.

He'd let them down horribly. It was almost as if he'd cheated to win the race. And since all three had dropped out one after another, expecting that he would as well, he had in a way won it unfairly. If everyone had run properly, Kirsty would almost certainly have won.

The victorious smile on Bill's face faded. He felt small and selfish and ungenerous. He felt ashamed.

But while Bill was standing, picking miserably at the embroidered roses on his pink frock, feeling quite rotten and wishing that everybody would stop cheering, Paul was still bravely pressing round the last bit of the circuit in his funny loping way. And he looked happy enough. He had a huge smile on his face. In fact, he looked positively radiant.

He threw himself across the finishing line, and lay like a tortoise on its back, beaming up at the sky.

'Second!' he yelled in triumph. 'I came second! *Second!*'

Everyone was cheering and clapping for Paul now.

Bill joined in, louder than anybody else.

'Hurray for Paul!' he yelled. 'Second!'

And he reached down to help Paul up.

Paul was a bit unsteady on his feet after the run. Whether it was excitement or exhaustion, Bill didn't know. But Mrs Collins took one brief look at Paul's thin, trembling legs, and said:

'That's it! That was the very last race! Well done, everybody!'

Happily they all trooped back towards the classroom. Astrid and Talilah came up on either side of Paul just in time to hear him confessing excitedly:

'I've never come second in a race before. *Never!*'

Kirsty came up behind Bill, and drew him quietly to one side.

'You just weren't listening, were you?' she scolded. 'Lying there on your back staring at clouds, away with the fairies. You were supposed to pretend to get a stitch!'

'I'm sorry,' said Bill.

'It doesn't matter,' Kirsty said. 'In fact it was probably all for the best. If he'd come first, Paul might have guessed.'

She turned to face him.

'It's just – ' Now, tipping her head to one

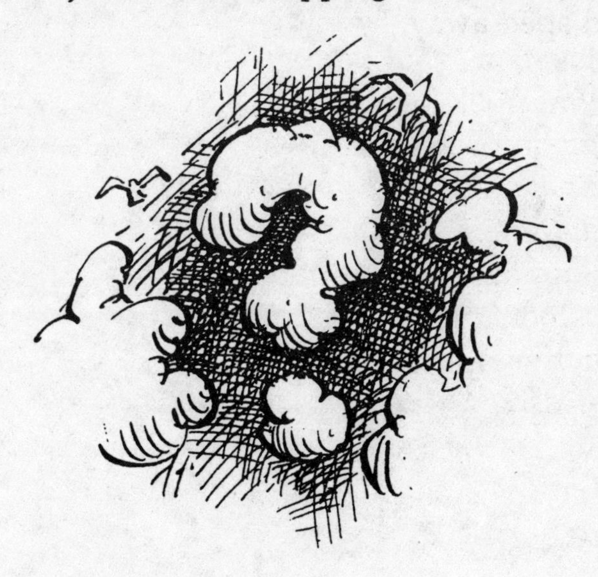

side, she looked him very closely in the eye. 'It's just –'

'What?'

Kirsty shook her head, sighing.

'It's just that somehow you seem *different* today. I can't think what it is about you that's odd. But you're not *you*.'

She turned to go.

Bill reached out to try to stop her.

'But who am I?' he asked her desperately. 'Who *am* I?'

But Kirsty, the fastest runner in the class, had sped away.

· 7 ·

Happy Ending

Maybe the day had been more tiring than he realised. Maybe the school work was harder than usual. Bill wasn't sure. All he knew was, he'd had enough. He wanted to go home. It had been the most horrible of days, and he'd be glad to have it over.

The clock hands seemed to crawl. Each

time he looked up, they had scarcely moved. The afternoon seemed endless – *endless*.

And then, at last, the bell rang. And after the usual shouting and clattering and slamming of desk lids, everyone made for the door.

As Bill went past her, Mrs Collins stretched out a hand to hold him back for just a moment.

'You're still not looking quite right to me,' she said. 'I can't work out what it is. But let's hope that you're your old self tomorrow!'

'Yes,' Bill agreed with her fervently. 'Let's hope!'

He had his doubts, though. And it was a dispirited Bill Simpson who trailed down the school drive, dragging his feet. At the gates, Paul was jumping up and down beside his baby sister's push-chair, excitedly telling his mother about the race. They smiled and waved, but Bill pretended not to see.

He was, it has to be admitted, in the worst

mood. He felt angry and bitter and resentful. And he was so sick of the silly pink frock that he would have liked the ground to open and swallow him.

But no such luck. In fact, worse was to come, it seemed. For there at the corner, nesting on one of the dustbins, was Mean Malcolm, waiting for his gang.

Mean Malcolm saw him coming, and whistled.

Bill looked a sight. He knew it. The frock was a rumpled mess, with grubby fingerprints all round the hem, a huge, brown football-shaped smudge on the front, paint smears down the folds, rips in each side where he had hunted in vain for pockets, a great criss-cross footprint where Rohan kicked him, and grass stains down the back – the sort of grass stains that *never* come out.

The frock was a disaster.

And that is probably why, when Mean Malcolm whistled at Bill Simpson again, he took it so very badly.

He stopped and glowered at Mean Malcolm.

'Whistling at *me?*'

Mean Malcolm looked astonished to find this pink apparition glaring at him with such menace. He shifted uneasily on the lid of his dustbin.

'*Because,*' continued Bill savagely, 'I am not a *dog!* I am – '

He hesitated a moment, not knowing quite how to finish; then yelled triumphantly:

'I am a *person!*'

And charging at Mean Malcolm with all the pent-up fury of the most horrible and frustrating day in his life, he flung him backwards off the dustbin lid, into a pile of spilled rubbish.

'There!' he yelled. 'That will teach you! Whistle at dogs in future – not at people!'

And he strode off towards home, a little more cheerful, leaving Mean Malcolm desperately trying to brush the carrot peelings and tea leaves off his purple

studded jacket before his gang came round the corner and saw him.

When Bill Simpson walked in the front door of his house, his mother was just coming in through the back door.

They met in the hall.

Mrs Simpson stopped in her tracks. She stared at Bill in absolute horror.

'Look at you!' she declared. '*Look* at you! What a mess! Fingerprints! Smudges! Paint smears! Rips! Footprints! Turn around!'

Obediently, Bill spun round. He heard his mother gasp.

'Grass stains!' she shrieked. 'The kind that *never* come out!'

Bill shrugged. It wasn't his fault, after all. He never *asked* to wear the silly frock.

Bill's mother sighed.

'You'd better take it off at once,' she said, unzipping the back and starting to undo the fiddly shell buttons. 'This is the last time I ever send *you* to school in a frock!'

She peeled the offending dress up over his head, and gave him a little push towards the stairs.

Bill needed no prompting. He ran up to his bedroom and pulled on a pair of jeans and a shirt.

Then he took the tiniest, sideways peep in his mirror.

And then another, slightly longer, peep.

And then a good, long stare.

He was a boy! Some people might have said that he could have done with a bit of a haircut . . . But he was definitely a boy.

Never in his whole life had Bill felt such relief.

Bella the cat came up and rubbed her soft, furry body around his ankles in the usual way. She didn't seem to notice any difference.

Bill picked her up and buried his face in her fur.

'It's all right,' he whispered to her delightedly. 'It's over. It's *over*. It doesn't matter if it was a dream, or not. *Whatever it was*, it's all over.'

She purred contentedly in his arms. He held her tight.

'And Mum says,' he repeated firmly to himself and Bella. 'That is the last time I *ever* go to school in a frock!'

And it was.

The Country Pancake

Chapter 1

In which we are introduced to Lancelot, Miss Mirabelle and Flossie the Cow

Lance sat on the wooden fence that ran round the meadow, watching the cows and worrying as usual about his teacher, Miss Mirabelle. Two feet away, Flossie his favourite burped gently, flicked her long raggedy tail, and watched him anxiously.

'It's no good, Flossie,' said Lance. 'Things aren't getting better. They are getting *worse*.'

Flossie shook her big heavy head and

looked, if possible, even more anxious than before.

'If she's not careful,' Lance warned, 'she's going to lose her job. She'll get the sack. Why, she spent almost half an hour this morning just staring out of the window sucking her pencil. There was practically a riot at the back of the classroom.'

Flossie turned round and ambled off towards the ragged bit of fence that was so good for back-scratching.

Left to himself, Lance sighed and stared up at the vast bowl of sky.

'She ought to try to do better,' he told the clouds above him. 'She's always writing it on other people's reports. She ought to try it herself. She should pull her socks up. She should get a grip. We can't go on like this. It's beyond a joke.'

Behind him another cow burped, rather more rudely than Flossie.

'All right for *you*.' Lance scowled. 'You never had to go to school. You don't know what it can be like.'

Lance remembered only too well

what school was like before Miss Mirabelle came. First there was Mr Rushman. Terrifying! He spoke so softly you could hardly hear, and then, as soon as you did something wrong because you hadn't heard, he shouted at you that you ought to listen. No one was sorry when he left the school.

Then there was Mrs Maloney. She seemed to think they were all idiots. She spoke so loud and clear and slow, and said everything she had to say at least a dozen times, and everything they did was so easy-peasy that everyone was driven half mad with boredom. There was great relief all round when Mrs Maloney moved back down to Infants.

Then there was Mr Hubert. He talked all the time. Nobody else got a word in edgeways. They never did anything. They just watched him talk. He talked about what they were going to do, but took so long talking they never did it. Then he broke both legs falling off his motorbike. They all signed the card to the hospital, but nobody cried. They just felt a little bit sorry for the nurses.

And then, like an angel, Miss Mirabelle came. One morning they were all fiddling about at their tables or hanging around the windowsills wondering who was going to take them, when in stepped a vision in a flowery dress, with golden hair piled high and tumbling down, and silver bell earrings that tinkled as she moved, and scarlet fingernails and bare brown legs. And on her dainty feet the vision wore the brightest, greenest shoes, with frills round the edges and bows on top, and the highest heels ever seen at Wallisdean Park School.

'I am Miss Mirabelle,' the vision said. 'Get off those windowsills. Stop fiddling about. Plonk your bums straight down on your little chairs, and listen to me.'

Extraordinary!

Half the class slid off the windowsills and crept to their seats. The other half stopped fiddling. There was absolute silence. You could have heard a pin drop. Everyone stared, wide-eyed and open-mouthed, as Miss Mirabelle hitched up her flowery skirts, perched on the very edge of the teacher's desk, crossed her legs elegantly at the knee, and told them:

'I am your new teacher, and I think I should tell you right at the start that I can stand practically anything in the world, but I can't stand *sniffers*.'

She reached in her capacious woven bag and pulled out a huge box of paper tissues.

'I'll put these here,' she said.

She placed the box ceremoniously on the front of her desk.

'At the first sign of a sniff, or a snuffle, or even a bit of a blocked nose, you are to come up here, take a tissue, and *blow*!'

She rose dramatically, and pointed to the cupboard at the back of the class-room.

'Sniffers will be sent to sit in there, out of sight and out of hearing. I'm

sorry, but there it is. I just can't help it. Sniffers bring out the *murderess* in me.'

Then suddenly she smiled, picked up the chalk, and, swinging round, began to write the date very neatly on the blackboard, just like any other teacher in the world.

Her back safely turned, everyone took the chance to glance at their friends, and nudge their neighbours. Deborah even whispered to Lance.

'What do you think of her?'

'She's different.' Lance shook his head. 'She certainly is different.'

And he was right. Miss Mirabelle certainly was different. She started the school day with a Wake You Up Sing Song. Her silver bell earrings tinkled when she laughed. And every so often during the morning she reached into her capacious woven bag and, pulling out an exquisite little pearl knife and an apple, she peeled off the skin in one long perfect coil, sliced up the apple thinly, and popped each delicate sliver into her perfect red mouth.

Lance watched. It made a change, he thought, from watching teachers mark books, or go round the class, or write on the board. Miss Mirabelle was different, she was exotic, she promised adventure. Lance longed for adventure, and he hoped she would stay.

But would she be able to stay different? Lance wasn't sure. He'd seen the headmistress take Miss Mirabelle aside after lunch, pointing first at Miss Mirabelle's high heels, then at the wooden floor in the hall. Mrs Spicer was worrying about pockmarks on her nice boards.

That's it for the shoes, then, thought Lance sadly. He knew Mrs Spicer's little talks. Mrs Spicer was a dragon. The high heels would end up in the bottom of Miss Mirabelle's closet. Tomorrow she'd be in flatties, or clumpies, like all the other teachers.

But she wasn't. The next day the amazing Miss Mirabelle turned up in the very same shoes.

The whisper ran round like wildfire.

'Wait till Mrs Spicer sees!'

Lance peeped at Miss Mirabelle. She didn't look worried. Cheerfully she called them into line and marched them smartly down the corridor towards the hall. But what would happen when Mrs Spicer saw her sail through the big swing doors wearing the same fancy shoes? Would Miss Mirabelle be told off? Sent out? Ordered home?

Lance was a bag of nerves. He imagined Mrs Spicer glancing up from her song book as the clatter of high heels came closer and closer along the corridor. He imagined her face darkening and her mouth drawing as tight as a purse string. He imagined her look of rage as Miss Mirabelle stepped on her precious wooden floor.

He was so nervous he would have liked to close his eyes as they went through the swing doors. Good thing he had to look to see where he was going. For otherwise he would have missed the sight of the amazing Miss Mirabelle reaching down, delicately

flipping off first one shoe, then the other, and dangling them elegantly from her fingertips as she picked her way barefoot across the hall, settled herself neatly on her canvas chair, looked up and smiled.

Mrs Spicer was livid. She was so furious she got the title of the song mixed up. She was so furious she lost her place twice in the prayer. She was so furious she stumbled on her clumpy shoes on her way out of the hall, leaving a scuff mark on her precious floor.

Miss Mirabelle smiled. Then she turned sweetly to her class.

'Come along, then,' she said. 'I think the show is over. Time to start on the work now.'

And that was another thing – the work. Work with Miss Mirabelle was different, too. Sometimes, when they were all doing something together, Miss Mirabelle would suddenly sigh, and complain:

'This is so boring. I am very bored.'

Often the class agreed. Someone would ask:

'Why do we do it, then?'

Miss Mirabelle would roll her eyes, and shrug.

'If you don't, you might grow up ignorant. I suppose being ignorant is even more boring than doing this.'

Sometimes they argued with her.

'This isn't boring.'

'It's not boring at all.'

'I'm really interested.'

'I could do this *all day.*'

Miss Mirabelle never minded them arguing. (That was another thing that made her different.) Sometimes she'd sit back and listen to what they had to say. Sometimes she'd look amazed, as if they were a pack of lunatics. Sometimes she'd simply lose interest, cup her head on her hands, and stare out of the window while the discussion turned into a riot around her.

Oh, she took some getting used to, did Miss Mirabelle. Admittedly she was nowhere near as terrifying as Mr Rushman, or as boring as Mrs Maloney, or as fond of her own voice as Mr Hubert. But she could certainly make them all jump. For one thing, she'd lied to them right at the start. She'd said she could stand practically anything in the world except sniffers, but it just wasn't true. There were a million things she couldn't stand. Hardly a day went by when Lance did not lean over the fence on his way home from school and, patting Flossie till the dust flew up in clouds, tell her:

'Miss Mirabelle can't *stand* people who lick their fingers before they turn over the pages of a book.'

Or:

'Miss Mirabelle can't *stand* people who snigger when someone says they have to go to the lavatory.'

Or:

'Miss Mirabelle can't *stand* people who fuss when a wasp flies in the classroom.'

Whatever it was Miss Mirabelle couldn't stand, Flossie would look as concerned as usual. Pushing her great head closer, she'd almost butt poor Lance off the fence.

'She hasn't much patience,' Lance confessed. 'She shouldn't really be a teacher. She's not quite right for the job. She went berserk when I forgot my gym shoes. She went mad when Deborah bent down the corner of her page, to mark her place. She took a fit when Ally dropped pencil sharpenings on the floor.'

He scratched Flossie's ears as hard as he could, to please her. Her hide was so tough that it was hard work.

'I'm not sure she'll keep the job,' he said sadly. 'Not if she doesn't change her attitude . . .'

The idea of Miss Mirabelle leaving filled him with gloom. He'd suffered Mr Rushman, and Mrs Maloney, and Mr

Hubert. He knew what school could be like.

It was as if Flossie wanted to shake him out of his black mood. She tossed her head, throwing poor Lance off balance once again.

'Really,' Lance insisted. 'Mrs Spicer has been suspicious of Miss Mirabelle ever since that business of the high-heeled shoes. She watches her terribly closely. Miss Mirabelle is in danger.'

He patted Flossie's flank and, not for the first time, wished with all his heart that Flossie had been born, not a cow, but a horse. Lance longed for a horse. He longed for adventure. He longed for unknown countries he could ride across, and dragons he could fight, and damsels in distress he could rescue. Oh, Lance loved Flossie. Of course he did. He'd loved her since he first saw her, twenty minutes old, lying in deep straw, steaming, with damp and curly hair, and the farmer said: 'Choose a name,' and Lance called out: 'Flossie!'

Then he had sat on the wooden bars

of the cow stall and watched as Big Buttercup licked her lovely new-born calf. After a bit, little Flossie began to struggle to her feet. Lance held his breath, willing her on. She tried so hard. Her spindly legs wobbled, letting her down time and again. But in the end she made it. Lance was thrilled. And with a bit of nudging from Big Buttercup's huge soft nose, the hungry little creature found the teat, wrapped her tongue around to get a grip, and sucked hard.

Lance went back day after day, to watch Flossie grow. He carried water and shovelled cow-cake for all the cattle on the farm, but Flossie was his favourite. He talked to her while she sniffed curiously at his pockets and butted him with her head to try and make him play, and followed him round the field. He told her everything, and kept on telling as the months went by, and Flossie grew and grew, till finally she was vast, enormous, bigger than Lance, almost as big as a car, with huge brown, anxious, motherly eyes.

So Lance loved her dearly. He always would. But she was only a cow. Cows weren't exotic. They weren't different. And they didn't promise adventure. You couldn't go righting wrongs, killing dragons, rescuing damsels in distress with a cow. Let's face it, cows aren't even very bright.

Oh, Lance could still tell all his troubles to Flossie. She was still perfect for that. But it would be foolish to expect any more.

He took the shortcut home across the meadow, jumping the big brown cowpats and singing the song his friends always sang when somebody careless put their foot in one.

'Which would you rather?
Run a mile,
Jump a stile,
Or eat a country pancake?'

He wasn't daft. Though he was hungry now, and ready for tea, he'd run the mile or jump the stile!

Chapter 2

In which Miss Mirabelle tells a Giant Whopper

Lance knew he was right to fear that Miss Mirabelle was in danger. You could tell from the look on Mrs Spicer's face that she was suspicious of her new teacher. She didn't like the way Miss Mirabelle made no effort to hide her yawns during assembly. She didn't like the fresh flowers Miss Mirabelle wore in her hair. She gave them such a poisonous look that Lance couldn't help expecting them to wilt. She put a firm stop to Miss Mirabelle's Wake You Up Sing Songs and frowned when she heard the high heels clattering down the corridor.

And sometimes she made surprise visits to the classroom. (She'd never done that before, even when Mr Rushman was terrifying them half to death, or Mrs Maloney was boring them stupid, or Mr Hubert's endless nattering was getting on their nerves.) She'd creep along the corridors, making no sound. Suddenly her head would appear behind the little square pane of glass set in the door.

Everyone's eyes would swivel round. Miss Mirabelle would notice at once.

'Fancy!' she'd say. 'A visitor! How very refreshing. We do welcome breaks.'

The door would open. Mrs Spicer would creep in, rubbing her hands.

'Don't let me interrupt you, Miss Mirabelle. I'll wait till you've finished. Please carry on, *exactly* as before.'

Miss Mirabelle would smile her sweet

smile, and turn back to the class.

'Where was I?' she'd ask.

Then, before anyone could tell her that she'd been admiring Melissa's tooth which was hanging only by a thread, or showing them photographs of her sister's wedding, or asking their advice on a name for her new kitten, she'd carry on, very firmly indeed:

'Oh, yes. As I was just saying, it's time to get out your workbooks and carry on, while I come round the class.'

She'd turn to Mrs Spicer, and spread her hands.

'Now,' she'd say angelically. 'How can I help you?'

She didn't always get away with it so easily. Mrs Spicer found sniffers in the cupboard several times, and wasn't very pleased. The whole class was spotted through the windows one day with their eyes firmly closed, after Miss Mirabelle discovered that rubbing her eyes very gently made a faint squelch. And then there were all the times Mrs Spicer walked past the room and, glancing in quickly, caught Miss Mirabelle with her head propped on her hands, staring out of the window while such a riot went on around her that no one even noticed the spy in the doorway.

Mrs Spicer would fling the door open.

'Miss Mirabelle?'

Everyone noticed her now. There was absolute quiet.

'Miss Mirabelle!' she'd call again, even more sharply.

Miss Mirabelle would give herself a little shake, and turn around slowly.

'Oh!'

She'd look astonished, as if it were not possible that she was really still sitting here in the classroom, with so many children around her. 'Sorry. I must have been miles away. I was having a daydream.'

And Mrs Spicer would close the door with a fierce little bang, to let Miss Mirabelle know that a classroom was no place for a daydream.

But Miss Mirabelle wasn't the only one to suffer from daydreams. Lance

spent hours staring into space, wondering how he could protect Miss Mirabelle from danger. He suspected Mrs Spicer of spending her days locked in her office secretly writing letters of complaint about Miss Mirabelle to important people.

Dear Head of the Governors,
Miss Mirabelle does not fit in at Wallisdean Park School. She hasn't the right attitude. Her clothes are too fancy, and her heels are too high. She spends far too much time staring out of the window, and holds eye-squelching sessions when she is bored.

On her very own admission, sniffers bring out the **murderess** *in her. I think she ought to go.*

Yours truly,
Emily Spicer

Lost in his daydreams, Lance thought what he'd do. He'd run like the very wind down to the meadow, where Flossie would be standing, her head lowered, cropping the fresh juicy grasses. But Flossie was strangely altered in his daydream. Her legs and neck were longer. Her body was nowhere near as bulky as usual. Muscles rippled beneath her glossy skin. Her head was a different shape. Only the lovely velvet-brown eyes remained the same. The rest of Flossie had become a beautiful and fleet-footed horse who whinnied with excitement and promised adventure.

Lance would scale the fence. Flossie would prance closer. Lance would make a flying leap on to her back, and she would clear the fence with a jump so high and wide and smooth and effortless, it was like flying.

He'd clutch her silken mane as they gathered speed along the country lane. Her delicate hooves would clatter as they spun along. Her tail would fly out behind.

But Mrs Spicer would be almost at the letter-box, her tell-tale letter in her outstretched hand. Would they be in time to rescue Miss Mirabelle?

Yes! Quicker than a lightning flash, Flossie would canter through. Hanging on to her mane for dearest life, Lance would lean down, and, reaching out, snatch the offending letter from the old dragon's hand.

'You *shan't* get rid of Miss Mirabelle!' he'd cry bravely. 'I shall save her!'

And ripping the mean little letter into a thousand pieces, he'd scatter it to the four winds as they rode home.

If only life itself were that simple! The weeks of term went by. Everyone's workbook filled up, and everyone moved on to a different-coloured reader. Miss Mirabelle certainly made them all work. But still Lance couldn't help worrying about her. It seemed to him that he couldn't walk down a corridor without seeing Mrs Spicer purse her lips, or raise her eyebrows, or give a cold little look of disapproval as the amazing Miss Mirabelle sailed by.

'It's getting worse,' he warned Flossie gloomily. 'Mrs Spicer is definitely out to get her. You wait and see.'

And Flossie didn't have to wait long. It wasn't more than another week before Lance came home from school one day dragging his feet, with his head hanging.

Flossie picked her way through the mud in the ditch and stuck her head over the wooden fence to greet him.

Lance took no notice. He just kept walking.

Flossie let out a loud, long, plaintive moo.

Lance turned and, noticing Flossie for the first time that afternoon, hurried back to climb the fence and slide his arms around her neck.

'Oh, Flossie!' he said. 'Guess what has happened.'

Flossie looked anxious.

'Miss Mirabelle has been so silly. She's in big trouble.'

Flossie pulled a hoof out of the mud with a great sucking sound, then put it back in exactly the same place.

Lance explained.

'You see, it's nearly Open Day, when each class does something special to make a bit of money.'

Flossie tilted her head.

'People from other classes keep coming up to us,' explained Lance, 'and asking, "What is your class doing this year?" '

He looked dismayed.

'And we can't *answer*.'

He spread his hands.

'Miss Mirabelle won't *choose*,' he told Flossie. 'She won't admit it, but I think she thinks the whole idea of making money is boring. She's very easily bored. So she keeps putting off the decision. We never *choose*.'

He patted Flossie on the neck, more to comfort himself than to comfort the cow.

'Everyone else chose *weeks* ago,' he said. 'Class One is going to run a little Bring-and-buy stall. Class Two is putting on a show in the hall. Class Three has organised a sponsored run. Even the Infants are making Spaceman

Snoopy collecting boxes out of old toilet roll holders and bits of tinfoil.'

He paused, sunk in gloom.

'And we've done *nothing*!'

Flossie rubbed her massive head against the fence. Clouds of dust flew up in Lance's face, but he was so preoccupied he didn't notice.

'And that's not the worst of it,' he told Flossie. 'Mrs Spicer has been popping in every day to ask Miss Mirabelle, "Have you decided yet?" And Miss Mirabelle just keeps answering, "No, not quite yet." You can tell Mrs Spicer is getting terribly suspicious. You see, she doesn't like Miss Mirabelle's attitude.'

He shook his head. Flossie shook hers.

'And this morning,' he told Flossie, 'Mrs Spicer lost her patience and stormed into our room. You could tell she was on the war-path. She asked Miss Mirabelle again.'

Flossie's huge, loving brown eyes were melting.

'And Miss Mirabelle panicked, and

told a lie! "Oh, yes," she said. "That's all fixed up now." '

Flossie blinked twice.

'Quite,' agreed Lance. 'A bare-faced lie! And Mrs Spicer didn't believe it, either. She saw us all sitting with our mouths open, and she asked Miss Mirabelle, as sweet as sugared poison, "And may I ask what, exactly, your class has decided to do?" '

Lance's face paled as he told his dear Flossie the worst of it.

'And Miss Mirabelle replied, "I'm afraid I can't tell you, Mrs Spicer. You see, it's a secret." '

Flossie let out a soft bellow of amazement.

'That's right,' said Lance. 'Miss Mirabelle told a giant whopper. She has no secret plan. She can't have. She doesn't have a plan at all!'

He slid down from the fence on Flossie's side, to take the shortcut home across the meadow.

'And with only just over a week left, she's not very likely to think of one, is

she?' he added bitterly.

Shades of the terrifying Mr Rushman and the boring Mrs Maloney rose up to haunt him. Perhaps even the dreaded Mr Hubert's broken legs had healed by now.

'We have to save her, Flossie!' he announced. 'We *must* save Miss Mirabelle from the dragon Spicer!'

On his way home, absorbed by anxiety and gloom, he put his foot right in a pancake.

Chapter 3

In which the Terrible, Terrible Secret hangs heavily over All

Miss Mirabelle came into school next morning in the worst mood. The clattering of her high heels coming closer down the corridor sounded as dangerous as machine-gun fire. She slammed the door shut behind her, hurled her capacious woven bag on to her desk, then put her hands on her hips.

She glowered round the class.

'Start thinking about this Open Day,' she told them.

Start thinking? What a *cheek!* Lance practically needed two matchsticks to keep his eyes propped open. He was exhausted. *Start* thinking? He'd been lying awake thinking all night!

'I thought you already had a plan,' Deborah said, mystified. 'You told Mrs Spicer it was all fixed up. You said it was a secret.'

The faintest blush rose on Miss Mirabelle's cheeks.

'I did have a bit of an idea,' she said, embarrassed. 'And, at the time, it seemed better to keep it a secret. But it wasn't much of an idea. And now I've forgotten it.'

She glanced round, as though daring them not to believe her.

'At least we've still got a secret,' giggled Deborah. 'It is a secret that we've got no plan.'

Miss Mirabelle wasn't amused. Sinking on to her chair, she buried her head in her hands.

'Oh, it's certainly a secret: a terrible, terrible secret. It's been hanging over me all night.'

And me, Lance thought privately.

Miss Mirabelle raised her head.

'Think,' she told all of them. 'We don't have much time. Think very *hard*.'

They all sat thinking hard. Every few minutes someone would shoot up a hand and make a suggestion. But no one came up with an idea Lance hadn't already thought of, and given up, because it was impossible –

'We could hire elephants from the zoo!'

Or another class was already doing it –

'We could put on a little show in the hall!'

Or it would take more than a week to organise –

'We could invite somebody famous, and sell tickets!'

The ideas were all hopeless. Miss Mirabelle got more and more miserable. She reached in her capacious woven bag and took out her little pearl knife and an apple. For the first time ever her hands

shook a little as she peeled, so that her usual perfect coil fell off in ragged chunks.

The class watched silently. They'd seen Miss Mirabelle bored, and they'd seen her cross-patch. They'd never seen her rattled. It made them nervous.

'Surely,' she kept saying, 'One of you can think of *something*.'

It seemed to Lance that she was

looking directly at him.

But no one could think of anything. The morning went from bad to worse. Miss Mirabelle fell into an even blacker mood. She was snapping at people for everything they did, then snapping at them for not doing anything. And she threatened Deborah with the cupboard for just breathing loudly, nothing like sniffing at all! After a bit Lance found himself beginning to wonder whether Miss Mirabelle deserved to be rescued. It was her own fault, after all. She should never have wasted all that time staring out of the window, or told that foolish Giant Whopper.

But he couldn't help wanting to help her, all the same. She was still the amazing Miss Mirabelle. She stood there in her brilliant yellow dress with golden sunflowers sewn on with gleaming beads. She was so exotic, so different (and so much of an improvement on Mr Rushman and Mrs Maloney, and the dreadful Mr Hubert). He couldn't help wanting to save her. He knew what school could be like.

And her black mood did not last long.

'Come on,' she said, after a while. 'Worrying is so *boring*. Let's have a change. Let's do some painting. You can all think while you paint, and we'll do our work later.'

She went to the cupboard and wheeled out the trolley with all the art supplies.

Lance took his sheet of paper and a brush. Flattening the paper in front of him, he stabbed his paintbrush into the first paint pot Miss Mirabelle handed him and took a look. It was bright green.

Without thinking, he swept his brush over the paper. And again . . . And again . . . The green was very green. It was like grass after a week of sun and showers. Lance drifted gently off into a daydream. Together, he and Flossie were pounding over the lush green grass of the meadow. They were off on an adventure – crossing the world to right wrongs, kill dragons, rescue damsels in distress.

He was paying no attention at all to his painting. He didn't even bother to change colours. He just kept sticking his brush into the pot in front of him. Gradually the whole sheet of paper was filling up green.

Just as he was imagining sweeping Miss Mirabelle up beside him on Flossie's strong back, out of the reach of the dragon, she surprised him by appearing in the flesh at his shoulder.

'What's that?' she asked, pointing.

Lance took a look at what he'd done. It was a sheet of paper painted green. That's all there was.

'It's a meadow,' Lance said quickly. (It was the only green thing that sprang to mind.)

Miss Mirabelle wasn't impressed.

'Real meadows don't look like that,' she scoffed. 'Real meadows aren't just solid green squares. They have weeds, and patches of mud, and fences and ditches. They have mole-hills and paths across them. And wild flowers, and cows.'

She sailed off, to look at someone else's work.

Lance scowled at her departing back. Really, when she was in this mood she wasn't a damsel worth rescuing at all.

'And cowpats,' he added rudely under his breath. 'Don't forget they have cowpats.'

And, reaching across, he stuck his paintbrush into one of the other pots, stabbed at his plain green square, and ground the brush round and round.

'There!' he said crossly. 'A real meadow.'

A splotch of cowpat brown sat right in the middle of his sheet of paper. One country pancake in a field of green.

Lance stared at it. And then he stared some more. Then some more. Inside his brain, a little idea was growing, growing, growing. An idea that grew, like Flossie the baby calf, until it was enormous. An idea big enough to save the day.

'Miss Mirabelle.'

Lance tiptoed towards her desk. She was sitting with her head cupped in her hands, staring out of the window.

'Miss Mirabelle,' he whispered. 'I have had an idea.'

Miss Mirabelle turned her head.

'An idea?'

She looked hopeful.

'Yes,' Lance said softly. 'I have an

idea. It's easy to arrange, and no one else would ever think of doing it.'

Her eyes lit up. Could it be possible?

'And,' Lance added proudly, 'it is exactly the sort of idea that really ought to be kept a secret.'

Miss Mirabelle's velvety-brown eyes were melting as she looked at him.

'Tell me,' she said. Excitedly, she pushed the box of tissues aside and patted the corner of her desk. 'Sit here and tell me your idea.'

'It's very *different*,' warned Lance. 'Some people might even think it was –' He paused, searching for the right word, and couldn't find it. He finished up: '– a bit *too* different.'

'Try me,' said Miss Mirabelle.

So Lance perched on the corner of her desk and told Miss Mirabelle his idea. As he explained, a little smile came on to her face for the first time that morning. It grew and grew, like his idea, until it was enormous.

'Brilliant!' she said, when he had finished. 'How did you think of *that*?'

She didn't wait for an answer. 'It is *amazing,*' she said. He could tell from the expression on her face that she was delighted. 'That is – ' She paused, searching for the right word, and couldn't find it.

'Different,' she finished up at last. 'That is certainly *different.*'

'Oh yes,' agreed Lance. 'It's different, all right.'

Miss Mirabelle turned to the class.

'We have been saved,' she announced.

'Lance here has had the most brilliant idea.'

Everyone stopped painting to listen. Miss Mirabelle pushed Lance forward.

'Go on,' she ordered. 'Tell everybody.'

So Lance explained his idea a second time. When he had finished there was a long, long silence. The whole class was staring at him. They couldn't believe it. Then, suddenly, someone at the back began to giggle. Just one person at first, and very softly. But soon there was another. And another. And another. And soon the whole class was rocking and laughing, and calling out excitedly.

'It's certainly *different*.'

'There'll be no trouble keeping it a secret. No one would ever dare tell Mrs Spicer!'

'*No one* will want to miss it. *Everyone* will come.'

'We'll make a fortune. Everyone will want a ticket!'

'It's brilliant. *Brilliant*.'

'Why has nobody ever thought of it before?'

'I know why!'

'So do I!'

Miss Mirabelle rose. The silver bell earrings tinkled as she cried out:

'Three cheers for Lancelot Higgins! Hip, hip, *hooray*!'

Mrs Spicer peeped through the little glass pane in the door just as they were cheering their heads off. Nobody even noticed.

'Hip, hip, hooray!'

'Good old Lance!'

'And his amazing cow!'

'Hip, hip, *hooray*.'

Chapter 4

In which Mrs Spicer sees a Great Improvement All Round, and is Delighted

Miss Mirabelle came into school the next morning with a smile on her face. She reached in her capacious woven bag and drew out several balls of knitting wool and a big box of brand new ice-lolly sticks.

She laid the balls of wool along the edge of her desk, and opened the box lid to show them the lolly sticks packed tightly inside.

'One thousand,' she said.'*Exactly*.'

Miss Mirabelle looked round at the sea of baffled faces.

'Now, listen carefully,' she said. 'It's going to be a busy day. Let me explain . . .'

Inside her office, Mrs Spicer sat staring at the sheet of paper on her desk. Printed across the top were the words:

Report on Miss Mirabelle

and nothing else.

Yet . . .

Mrs Spicer was thinking. She was thinking hard. She knew exactly what she thought of Miss Mirabelle. Oh, yes. She knew exactly what she'd like to write. She just wasn't absolutely sure it was quite fair to give anyone, even the amazing Miss Mirabelle, such a terrible report without checking one last time.

She'd creep along. And if Miss Mirabelle was sitting with her head cupped in her hands, staring out of the window while a riot went on around her . . . Or if Miss Mirabelle was peeling an apple with her exquisite pearl knife while everyone watched the skin falling in one long perfect coil . . . Or if there were sniffers in the cupboard . . . Then Mrs Spicer would write her report. Yes! Every last word!

Furtively she tiptoed along the corridor. As she came closer she heard Miss Mirabelle's clear voice echoing from the classroom. But was she teaching them anything? Or was she, as usual, just admiring somebody's wobbly tooth, or showing them photographs of her sister's new-born baby, or asking their advice on the best kitty litter?

But, no! It sounded as if, just for once, she'd actually caught Miss Mirabelle giving a lesson. How very strange!

'If there are twenty-five of you,' Miss Mirabelle was saying, 'And I have exactly one thousand lolly sticks, how many should I give to each of you, to make it fair?'

Miss Mirabelle made it sound as if it really was a problem. What a good way of making division sound interesting – lolly sticks! Mrs Spicer eavesdropped with interest as the whole class struggled aloud with the sum. They all seemed very keen to get it right, as though no one wanted too many, or too few.

Then out the answer popped:

'We get exactly forty each! And there'll be none left over!'

'Good. That will be all fair then,' Miss Mirabelle said. And she sounded as if it really mattered. Mrs Spicer was astonished. She made her way silently back to her office and sat in front of the paper, bewildered. What was she going to do now? She might be a bit of a dragon, but she was always scrupulously fair. She couldn't write a dreadful report on Miss Mirabelle after overhearing that simply splendid lesson in division. She'd have to put the report aside for a little while. Catch Miss Mirabelle out later . . .

Just before break, Mrs Spicer tried again. She slunk along the corridor,

making no sound. No sound came from Miss Mirabelle's room, either. Perhaps they were all busy, Mrs Spicer thought, with one of their little eye-squelching sessions . . .

Mrs Spicer peeped through the pane of glass set in the door. Amazing! She could scarcely believe her eyes! The whole class was working hard, even that little daydreamer, Lancelot Higgins! Everyone's head was bent over their desk. Everyone was concentrating. Usually, when Mrs Spicer peeped into a classroom, at least one person would be staring idly around, and look in her direction, and notice her at once.

Not here. Not today. Today they were all so busy that no one looked up. Mrs Spicer couldn't make out exactly what they were doing. It *looked* as if they were writing numbers neatly on the ends of brand-new lolly sticks, but that was ridiculous. They must have been doing something else. But, no doubt about it, they were certainly working.

Shaking her head in disbelief, Mrs

Spicer turned and went back down the corridor. She had better get back to her office. That report on Miss Mirabelle had to be posted today. But still, it was difficult to write the report she wanted to write after seeing the class working so well and so busily.

It would be better to wait till after break. She'd feel more like it then.

A few minutes after the bell rang to signal the end of break-time, Mrs Spicer pushed aside her coffee cup. Time to write the report! She was just glancing out of the window as she reached for her pen, when she happened to notice the children from Miss Mirabelle's class gathering around the football pitch.

Mrs Spicer studied her watch. Well, really! Break-time ended at least ten minutes ago. What could Miss Mirabelle be thinking of, letting her class wander about all over the place? This would go straight in the report!

But what were they doing? Extraordinary! They were working. No doubt about it. They were working hard. With metre sticks and a long tape-measure, the class was busy measuring along the sides of the football pitch and dividing each side into smaller equal lengths.

Mrs Spicer's writing hand trembled. She had to write the report. She had to write it today. She knew what she wanted to write. She was desperate to write it and get rid of the amazing Miss Mirabelle and her high heels for ever. But what she was seeing outside made it impossible for her to write Miss Mirabelle a bad report. It simply wouldn't be fair. How many teachers can make measuring a rectangle interesting for children? Not very many. Using the football pitch was such a fine idea! Mrs Spicer couldn't help feeling a little bit pleased with Miss Mirabelle as she stared out of the window. She'd have to put off the report till after lunch.

But after lunch things were no worse. In fact, they were even better. Mrs Spicer could scarcely believe it. There were the children from Miss Mirabelle's class, outside again, fanning along the sides of the football pitch. What did they have in their hands? Knitting wool? Yes. How extraordinary! What on earth were they doing?

Mrs Spicer leaned her forehead against the cool glass of her window-pane and watched, fascinated, as the children from Miss Mirabelle's class carefully divided the entire football pitch into exactly equal squares, one thousand of them, and marked them out with wool. Wonderful! The most interesting way of measuring area that Mrs Spicer had ever seen. Why hadn't she thought of teaching it that way herself? Really, she ought to take Miss Mirabelle aside in the staff room next time she saw her and tell her what a splendid idea it was. Excellent! Excellent! So much better than just doing it in the dreary old workbooks!

And what were they all doing now?

How strange! They were all kneeling down and pushing a little marker like a lolly stick into each square. How clever! Now every square was measured out

exactly and marked with one of those numbered lolly sticks. And there were exactly one thousand!

What a splendid lesson!

Mrs Spicer couldn't help it. When she saw sloppy teaching, she got annoyed. And when she saw splendid teaching, she was delighted. Drawing the sheet of paper towards her, she unscrewed the top of her fountain pen, and wrote.

Report on Miss Mirabelle
I must confess that when Miss Mirabelle first came to teach at Wallisdean Park School I did have doubts. Eye-squelching sessions . . . Sniffers in the cupboard . . . And those shoes! But recently I have seen a great improvement all round. Not everyone can make an interesting class out of division, or measuring rectangles, or working out areas. Mr Rushman couldn't. Nor could Mrs Maloney or Mr Hubert. But Miss Mirabelle can. She uses lolly sticks, and balls of wool – even the football pitch. She is amazing and I am delighted.

Yours very truly.
Emily Spicer

There. That would do. It was a fine report, and Miss Mirabelle deserved it. Yes! Every last word!

Mrs Spicer folded the sheet of paper, slid it inside the envelope and sealed the flap. She glanced at her watch again. Time for the post.

She walked towards the door, holding the letter in her hand. And for the first time ever when thinking about Miss Mirabelle, Mrs Spicer was smiling. A little melody she'd overheard the children singing in the playground floated into her mind, and she began to hum. What were the words?

Which would you rather?
Run a mile?
Jump a stile?
Or eat a country pancake?

Really it was a very sweet little song, compared with a lot of the rather tasteless rubbish one heard them bellowing at playtime. Mrs Spicer sang it to herself all the way home and for most of the evening.

Chapter 5

In which Lance's Granny is Totally Disgusted

The farmer was astonished. She dropped the end of the hose-pipe she was dragging across the courtyard and stared at Lance.

'You want to borrow a *cow*?'

Lance stared at the water scudding in silky waves across the cobbles.

'Yes, please,' he answered politely. 'Just for the afternoon. She'll be back in time for milking.'

'A *cow*,' said the farmer meditatively.

'Fancy a cow! I'm often asked for a horse. Never a cow.'

'Well,' Lance said, a shade uneasily. 'This is a bit different.'

'It certainly is,' said the farmer. 'What do you want a cow for?'

Lance looked down and inspected the ends of his shoes. They were muddy from the water spilling out of the hose-pipe. This was the moment he'd been dreading. It hadn't been too bad, whispering the idea into Miss Mirabelle's ear in the classroom. That hadn't been too difficult. And it hadn't been all that hard, either, explaining it to everyone else in the class. They'd just sat wide-eyed, listening quietly (until the giggling began, of course).

Telling the farmer was not quite so easy. Lance found it impossible to describe exactly why he wanted to borrow a cow.

'Oh, just to sort of walk about a bit.'

'Just sort of walk about a bit?'

'Yes. On our school football pitch.'

The farmer was mystified.

'But what's the *point*?'

Lance gave up inspecting the ends of his shoes and took to inspecting his fingernails instead.

'People will probably be standing around the pitch,' he offered finally, after a long struggle for words. 'Sort of watching.'

'Sort of watching? Sort of watching *what*?'

'The cow.'

'But *why*?'

Lance shrugged, as if that part of things were no concern of his.

'Well, really, just to see where she goes, I expect.'

The farmer shook her head.

'I don't know,' she said. 'I'm glad I don't have any children. I'm sure I'd worry myself silly about what they do all day in school.'

She reached down for the end of her hose-pipe.

'Well, Lance,' she said, 'you've spent whole weeks helping me. So you can borrow a cow for one afternoon. But it will have to be Flossie. Flossie knows you, and Flossie is calm and sensible. Flossie won't mind.'

'I'm sure no cow would *mind,*' Lance said eagerly. 'Our football pitch must be like Sunday dinner to a cow. All lovely and rich and green and luscious.'

'I can't think why you want a cow wandering about on it, then,' said the farmer. 'Before you know where you are, you'll be having to run after her with a shovel!'

She took off to the barn, dragging the hose. If she'd looked back, she might have seen Lance standing there in the courtyard hugging himself and grinning, before he too took off towards the meadow.

Flossie was lying in the meadow, chewing the cud. Lance slipped through the bars of the fence and strode over towards her. Most of the other cows in the herd got up and walked away as he came closer, but Flossie didn't bother.

Lance sat cross-legged on the grass in front of her.

'Hello, Flossie.'

Chewing, she gazed into his eyes. He gazed back into hers. They were enormous, as dark and gleaming as the beautiful old polished furniture in Granny's house.

'Flossie,' said Lance. 'It's about Saturday.'

He'd known her all her life. He loved her dearly. He couldn't just spring this on her. He had to explain.

'The thing is,' said Lance, 'I need your help.'

Flossie kept chewing, imperturbably.

Lance spread his hands.

'It's an odd thing to ask anyone to do,' he admitted openly. 'Even a cow.'

Her great jaws ground away steadily at the green spinachy cud. She didn't seem at all bothered.

'I wouldn't ask you if I had a choice,' said Lance. 'To be honest, I wish she'd picked another cow entirely. I wish she hadn't chosen you. But she says you're calm and sensible . . .'

He watched her closely.

'And she says you won't mind.'

Flossie swung her great head round and stared out thoughtfully over the meadow. Lance wondered what she was thinking. What did cows think about? Did cows think at all?

Not really, he decided. They couldn't think like people can. Oh, they could feel. They could feel pain if they got a thorn impacted in one of their hooves, or if nobody milked them, or if they broke a leg.

And they could feel satisfaction if they had a long drink of water on a hot day, or found a good bit of fence to scratch on.

And they could follow their instincts enough to gather at the corner of the field when it was milking time, and find their way to their own stalls.

But Flossie couldn't think the same way Lance could think. And she couldn't have such complicated feelings. She wouldn't feel excited about something that was going to happen, and she wouldn't fret afterwards if it went wrong. Cows had no imagination. That's why they were so peaceful, Lance thought. They didn't spend their days, like he did, chewing over yesterday and tomorrow. They just chewed the cud.

It was a pretty cushy life, when you came to think about it. No worries. Water on tap. Salt-licks tied to the fence. Constant meals. Nice warm barn. No fears for the future. No reason why a cow shouldn't be expected to be a bit of a help every now and again, when opportunity offered.

Lance rose to his feet, decided.

'So you'll help, won't you, Flossie? You won't mind?'

Flossie burped contentedly. The sweet smell of fermenting cud wafted over Lance. He waved it away.

Flossie struggled to her feet, startled.

'Don't bother to get up,' said Lance. 'I'm leaving anyway. But I'll be back to fetch you on Saturday.'

He paused, still a tiny bit anxious about the arrangement. There was one more small thing he felt he really should get clear.

'I do hope you understand how serious all this is,' he said gravely to Flossie. 'Almost all of the squares of the football pitch have been bought in the raffle. So we *must* have a winner.' He caught Flossie's eye. 'You mustn't just come and wander round the football pitch and nothing else.

You mustn't let me down.'

As if deeply offended at the very suggestion that she might fail in her charitable duty, Flossie swung round, turning her back on him. Delicately raising her tail, she left a huge fresh deposit practically at his feet before indifferently ambling off.

Lance looked down at the great steaming pancake, two inches from his shoes. Then he looked up and grinned. And calling after Flossie who was disappearing between the trees, he added his last stern warning:

'Mind now, Flossie! I'm taking that as a definite *promise*!'

'A raffle!' said Granny. 'Lovely. I adore raffles. May I buy a ticket?'

Lance dug in his pocket and drew out the last of the lolly sticks. They had been selling like hot cakes all week.

'Here,' he said. 'I saved the last five for you. Twenty pence each.'

Granny took the lolly sticks and inspected them curiously.

'A bit odd,' she said. 'Not like your common or garden raffle ticket.'

'They stick in the ground well,' Lance assured her.

Granny found herself eyeing Lance rather carefully.

'I'm glad your term is nearly over,' she said. 'Sometimes I worry that school is all too much for you.'

Lance couldn't think what she was on about. He carried on explaining about the lolly sticks.

'They have to stick in the ground,' he said. 'To mark the raffle squares. We read the number on the lolly stick when Flossie has chosen.'

'Flossie?'

'You know Flossie,' Lance said. 'Flossie the cow.'

Granny narrowed her eyes.

'A cow is picking the winner? A *cow*?'

'Yes,' Lance said. 'It's all arranged. It was my idea.'

Granny reached out a hand and laid it thoughtfully on Lance's forehead.

'I'm wondering if I should take you

home,' she said. 'I'm not absolutely one hundred per cent certain you ought to be out of bed.'

Lance realised suddenly that Granny thought he was unhinged.

'I'm perfectly all right,' he assured her. 'I haven't gone potty. Flossie will choose the winner.'

'Oh yes? Is she going to dip her hoof in a tub?'

'Of course not,' said Lance. 'She's going to do it differently. She's going to –'

He broke off. However many times he tried to describe the process, this bit was always difficult. He had no trouble imagining it himself. In his own mind the picture was perfectly clear. It was like one of his daydreams. Flossie became as sleek and powerful as the most valuable Arabian mare. She wore a bridle studded with precious jewels that glittered fiercely in the harsh sunlight. Astride her rode Lance himself, high in the saddle. He wore a suit of the richest velvet, a cap with a feather and a silver sword. Upon his saddle was emblazoned the royal crest that proclaimed his princely ancestry.

Tall, noble, handsome . . . When he rode through the gate into the field the crowds went mad, cheering wildly, hurling their hats in the air, dropping to their knees in wonder, fainting from the sheer excitement of the day.

Three times around the field of green they rode, he and Flossie, until at last the waiting crowd fell silent, gasped –

'Lance?'

Granny was looking quite anxious.

'Lance? Are you all right, dear?'

Lance pulled himself together.

'Sorry. I was just off in a daydream.'

Hastily Granny gathered up her jacket and her bag. She had decided it was best to take her grandson home and leave him in his parents' care. Obviously he was a bit feverish.

As they walked down the lane, hand in hand, the sight of all the cows in the meadow reminded Granny of what they had been talking about before Lance

suddenly went peculiar.

'About this raffle, Lance. Explain to me again. How is the cow going to pick the winner?'

Lance tried to pick his words carefully. But it was no use. Granny stopped dead in her tracks.

'Lancelot Higgins! I am totally *disgusted!*'

Furiously blushing, Lance stared ahead.

All the way home, Granny went on about it. 'Disgraceful . . . don't know what the schools are coming to . . . read in the papers . . . I blame the teachers, frankly . . . wouldn't dream of such a thing in my day . . . totally disgusted.'

Lance just kept walking.

As they reached the front gate, Granny stopped muttering and laid her hand on his.

'I won't come in. I'll say goodbye here.'

Lance hung his head.

Granny lifted his chin.

'Lance? Haven't you forgotten something?'

Dutifully, he raised himself on tiptoes, to be kissed.

'No, not that,' Granny said impatiently. 'You've forgotten to give me my lolly sticks for the raffle.'

Lance stared.

'But I thought that you were totally disgusted!'

Now it was Lance's Granny's turn to blush.

'And so I am. But I'm not going to miss a good raffle.'

A little shyly, Lance dug in his pockets and drew out the five lolly sticks he had so carefully saved for her all week.

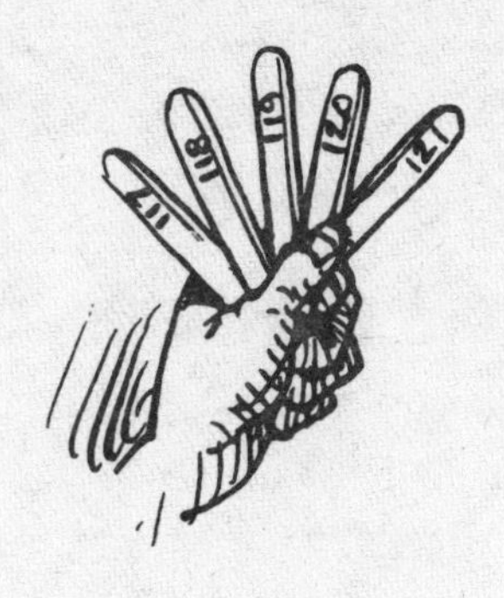

Shyly, Granny dug in her purse and gave him a pound.

'There,' she said. 'Wish me luck.'

'Good luck.'

Granny kissed him again, properly this time.

'You, too,' she laughed. 'You may need all the luck that you can get. What will you do if Flossie lets you down?'

Lance grinned.

'I don't know,' he teased. 'Run a mile? Jump a stile?'

Before she could reach out to put her hand over his mouth and stop him finishing the rhyme, he was safely up the path.

Chapter 6

In which we all watch Dear Flossie Save the Day

The farmer led Flossie out of the barn. Around her neck was a silken red cord with a tassel at each end.

'It's my dressing-gown belt,' said the farmer. 'I thought you'd like Flossie to look nice for the occasion.'

'She looks beautiful,' Lance said. 'She always does.'

Flossie tossed her head proudly.

'Off we go, then,' said the farmer. She slapped Flossie's rump hard. Not a speck of dust flew up.

'You've groomed her!' cried Lance.

The farmer shrugged.

'Flossie's Big Day,' she said, lifting the gate latch. 'And I must say I shall be glad when it's over. An awful lot of people seem to have chosen this week to stroll up my lane and have a good peer in my meadow.'

'What on earth for?'

'Search me. But I bet you have quite a few dung pat experts watching this raffle.'

She watched as Lance led Flossie carefully into the lane. She followed a few yards behind, ready to warn any traffic to slow down, but no cars came along before Lance reached the fork in the lane and turned down the narrow path that led to the football pitch.

So many people! Milling everywhere! It seemed as if everyone in the village had come along to Open Day, and brought all their friends. Even as he watched, more people spilled out of the school hall, after the end of the show.

The Bring-and-buy stall was practically sold out already. The Sponsored Runners were just running back. Even the Infants had stopped collecting in their Spaceman Snoopy boxes, for fear the weight of cash inside would damage them.

Suddenly Lance and Flossie were spotted.

'There's the cow!'

'Raffle time!'

Everyone gathered around the edge of the football pitch, some frantically searching their pockets for lolly sticks, some brandishing lucky mascots, some loudly admiring Flossie's fancy leading rein.

'Just what I need for my dressing-gown,' said Old Mr Hogg as soon as he saw it. 'Do you suppose I could get one from an agricultural supplier?'

Lance looked around. Had *everyone* bought a lolly stick? There was Mrs Spicer, clutching a handful and looking a little bemused. There beside her was Miss Mirabelle, holding a few more and

looking striking in a slinky black dress. There was the janitor, and the school governors. And Granny in the corner, waving excitedly. And his parents behind her.

Lance took a few steps forward. Tugging a little on the silken cord, Flossie followed.

The whispers ran around the football pitch –

'Keep your voices down!'

'Hush, now!'

'Musn't worry the cow!'

– until there was absolute quiet.

Lance's big moment. He musn't muff it now. This was the stuff of his day-dreams – the time when, with grace and skill and dignity, he would lead Flossie out on to the football pitch to launch his extraordinary raffle. It was everything he dreamed about. It was exotic. It was different. It was –

Why was Deborah running up to him, while everyone watched?

'Here,' she said, her clear voice carrying easily the entire length of the pitch. 'Miss Mirabelle said I was to give you this.'

It was a shovel. A great big rusty-edged shovel. Not different. Not exotic. Not at all the stuff of daydreams.

'Thank you,' said Lance. (His voice was frosty cold.)

'Go *on,* then,' said Deborah. '*Take* it.

It's *heavy*.'

Lance had no choice. He had to take it. And he could not walk Flossie back to the edge of the pitch, to dump it neatly out of sight between the bystanders' legs. He was just stuck with it.

And that's how it came about that the famous photograph of Lancelot Higgins that everyone saw in their newspapers the next morning showed him leading his cow so proudly into the middle of the football pitch waving a shovel to the cheering crowds.

'Let her go!'

'Take off the leading rein!'

'Leave her to wander!'

Lance tugged at the knot in the dressing-gown cord. It slid undone. He pulled the cord over Flossie's huge head.

Flossie mooed softly, and butted Lance gently in the belly with her head.

Lance leaned forward and tickled her behind both ears.

'Off you go, Flossie,' he whispered. 'Sunday lunch one day early. Eat up.

Feel free to go anywhere you want, do whatever you feel like doing. Make yourself at home.'

He added one last little plea.

'And don't let me down!'

Then he took off for the edge of the pitch, for fear that the crowd would accuse him of cheating.

Flossie looked round. People. She wasn't interested in people. She looked down. Grass. Oh, she was interested in grass. It had a few funny little wooden sticks poking up out of it, but they didn't bother her. It was fine grass, and ripe for chewing.

Keeping her eyes forever on the move for the next good patch, Flossie moved off across the football pitch.

Around the edge a hundred conversations took up again softly.

'How much is the prize?'

'Fifty pounds!'

'One thousand squares, though. At twenty pence a square. Why, that's –'

The crowd struggled with the sum.

Mrs Spicer was first.

'Why!' she declared to Miss Mirabelle. 'That's two hundred pounds!'

Miss Mirabelle was busy struggling with her high heels which kept sinking deeply into the soft ground, making her look rather unbalanced and peculiar.

'What?' she said. 'Oh yes. That's right. Fifty pounds for the winner, and the rest for the school.'

Mrs Spicer was thrilled.

'One hundred and fifty pounds!' she repeated. 'I could buy all those new maths books!'

Miss Mirabelle made a little face.

Mrs Spicer was quite excited now.

'And what exactly is the cow going to do, to choose the winning square?'

Perhaps Miss Mirabelle, struggling with her disappearing heels, did not take quite the care she ought to have done to choose her words.

'Flossie? Oh, she's just supposed to drop a giant pancake.'

'Drop a giant pancake?'

'That's right.'

Mrs Spicer was appalled. Truly

appalled. People who eavesdropped offered the opinion quite freely afterwards that, had she suffered from a weak heart, she might have died on the spot.

But Miss Mirabelle, still hauling her heels out of the mud, was paying no attention to the look on Mrs Spicer's face.

'Let's just hope the whole lot plops straight on one square,' she was saying. 'I can't imagine the trouble we'll have if it spreads over several. People will want us to weigh it, I shouldn't wonder, to get their fair share of the prize money.'

As one heel shot out of the mud without warning, the other sank deeply in again.

'I've done my best,' Miss Mirabelle went on irritably. 'Brushed up on *Proportion* in the maths books, and given Lance a shovel.'

'A shovel . . .'

Mrs Spicer felt faint. Could all these people – even the governors! – be standing here waiting to see where a cow –

Oh, it didn't bear thinking about! Mrs Spicer's voice was thick with danger as she asked Miss Mirabelle:

'And may I ask, dear, whose idea this is?'

There! Both heels out at last! Miss Mirabelle looked up. Mrs Spicer was staring at her with hostile, beady eyes. Her face was quite ashen. Was the old dragon annoyed? Really, some people were impossible to please. A hundred and fifty pounds in the school's pocket, and she was fussing about a little cow-pat!

Better not get poor little Lancelot Higgins in trouble, though. He'd been a poppet, and worked so hard. The very last thing Miss Mirabelle wanted was to reward him with a great row from Mrs Spicer.

She'd better take the blame herself.

'Oh, this whole raffle was all my idea.'

Behind her she thought she heard a little gasp of shock. She spun around. Lance Higgins was staring at her, open-mouthed. She was about to give him a little nudge and a wink, to try to explain to him why she had taken it upon herself to claim his brilliant idea for her own, when, all round the pitch, there was a sudden ripple of excitement.

Forgetting Lance, Miss Mirabelle turned back to see what was happening.

Oh, good old Flossie! She was coming up trumps! Head in the wind, tail raised triumphant, she was picking a winner!

'Hurrah!'

'Yippee!'

'Well done, Flossie! Well done!'

The crowd roared its approval. A dozen people ran across the pitch to check the lolly stick that marked the square.

'Four hundred and twelve!'

Waves of excitement ran around the pitch, as everyone checked their own lolly sticks, and those of their neighbours.

'Old Mr Hogg!'

'The winner!'

'No need to go searching for a new cord now, eh, Hogg? Get yourself a brand new dressing-gown!'

Old Mr Hogg stumbled forward. Before Mrs Spicer realised what was happening, Miss Mirabelle had thrust a fifty pound note into her hand.

'The presentation!'

'Speech! Speech!'

'Vote of thanks!'

Lance didn't stay to hear any speeches. Or any votes of thanks. Or any more hurrahs. He didn't stay to clear up after Flossie with the shovel, either. If this whole raffle was all her idea, then let Miss Mirabelle shovel up the cowpat!

He was *finished* with Miss Mirabelle anyway. She might still be better than the terrifying Mr Rushman, or the boring Mrs Maloney, or the dreadful Mr Hubert; but she was a bit *too* amazing for Lancelot Higgins.

Stealing his idea! What an exotic *cheek*!

Lance crept away, past Granny telling the governors how shocked she was by modern teaching methods. (She'd have been singing a very different tune, he knew, if she'd won the raffle.) He went past the janitor, and threaded his way between other people's parents, until he found himself beside the farmer, who was tethering Flossie.

'Can I walk her home?'

'Oh please, Lance. I should get back to work.'

This time she went ahead, to warn the traffic. Lance strolled behind, with Flossie. He didn't want to be a wet blanket and spoil her big day, but he couldn't help telling her what he was thinking.

'I'm *finished* with Miss Mirabelle. She's on her own now. She can look after herself. She can right her own wrongs, and kill her own dragons, and get her own damselly self out of her own distress.'

Flossie mooed sympathy and agreement as she clopped along.

'Cheek!' Lance was muttering, patting her neck for comfort. 'What is so

special about Miss Mirabelle anyway? That's what I'd like to know. She isn't all *that* amazing. Anyone can wear fancy clothes and peel a silly apple. Anyone can start up a Sing Song. No one can stand sniffers. And it's just plain stupid to try walking in high heels around a football pitch!'

He stopped at the gate and looked deep into Flossie's beautiful velvet eyes.

'You're not exotic,' he confessed. 'You're not different. You don't promise adventure. Let's face it, Flossie, you're not even very bright. But I can tell all my troubles to you. And I love you dearly. You're more amazing than Miss Mirabelle any day. And you make really good country pancakes!'

Pleased to be back with the herd, Flossie trotted off into the meadow, tossing her head.

Pleased to be nearly home, Lancelot followed her.

The Angel of Nitshill Road

'And the angel did wondrously . . .'
Judges, 13

1
Until the angel came . . .

Until the angel came, there were three terribly unhappy children at Nitshill Road School: Penny, Mark and Marigold. Shall we take Penny first?

Penny was plump. If you weren't friends with her, you might even say that she was getting on for fat. She had a pretty face, and lovely hair, and she was bright enough in class. But as the hands of the clock rolled round towards playtime she'd get a horrible feeling, as if her stomach was being gripped by a hard, invisible hand. However boring the lesson was, she wanted it to go on for ever and ever. Inside the classroom she was safe. Outside, Barry Hunter might go wheeling past, his arms stuck out like jet-plane wings, making the usual big show of having to swerve to avoid her.

'Beware of the mountain! Danger! Danger! The moving mountain is coming this way!'

'He's just stupid,' said Lisa, her friend. 'Ignore him.'

'You must treat him with the contempt he deserves,' said her father.

'Some people are just born pig-ignorant,' said her gran.

But Penny still felt terribly unhappy.

And so did Mark. Mark was small for his age. He had strange sticky-up hair, and he wore glasses thick as bottle-ends. He gnawed his fingernails and his pencils, and fussed and fidgeted, and even when he finally stopped racketing around the classroom and tried to sit down and work (not very well), he still got on everyone's nerves. But only Barry Hunter knew how to push him and push him and push him, till he flew into a temper.

'Mark the Martian!' he'd call from behind, imitating the rather peculiar stiff way Mark walked.

'Bionic eyes!' he'd shout, swooping up and peering through the thick lenses of Mark's spectacles.

'Controls not working properly?' he'd jeer, whenever Mark dropped a ball, or missed a kick, or ran into a wall by mistake.

And, sooner or later, unless the bell rang in time, Mark lost his temper – not like you or me, just getting red in the face and yelling, 'Oh, shut up, Barry Hunter! You're so stupid!' No. Mark went haywire, right out of control. With tears of rage spurting behind his glasses, he'd scream and howl and rush at Barry Hunter, trying to tear chunks of his hair out. Everyone turned to stare at him clawing and kicking and yelling. Some grinned quietly to themselves, but Barry Hunter laughed out loud. He was so big, he could hold Mark at arm's length and watch him flailing about like a windmill in a high gale. Then he'd tease him some more.

'Now, now, now! Temper, temper!'

Mark's elder sister said:

'Just stay right away from him, Mark. Then maybe he won't bother you.'

The teachers said:

'Really, Mark brings a lot of it on himself. He has to learn a bit of self-control. They'll have to sort themselves out.'

Mark's mother said:

'I'm going up to see the school if it doesn't stop.'

It didn't stop.

The third child was Marigold. Nobody knew that Marigold was unhappy. She never looked particularly sad, but then again, she never looked particularly happy. In fact, she never looked anything. A portrait painter would have had no trouble at all with Marigold. Her face never cracked into a smile, or darkened with a scowl. People had tried to make friends with her but they never got very far. She'd be away from school for a whole week, but only shrug when you asked what had been wrong with her. She'd hear your secrets, but she'd never tell you hers. In fact, come to think of it, she hardly ever spoke, even when Mr Fairway sighed over her

slipshod and unfinished work, or Barry Hunter and his gang tormented her in the playground.

'Where do you live, Marigold? Is it that smelly street you walk down after school?'

Marigold didn't answer. Others did.

'Push off, Barry Hunter,' said some of the girls. 'Leave Marigold alone. Don't be so mean.'

'You don't exactly live in a palace yourself,' said the others.

But when the girls turned to smile at Marigold, she'd simply drift away, not even saying thanks. What was the point of sticking up for someone who doesn't care? You might as well leave her alone and get on with your own games.

'She can always join in if she wants,' they said to one another.

'She doesn't mix at all,' the teachers said.

'I'd try and do something about it,' said the head teacher. 'But, honestly, she doesn't seem all that unhappy. I'm sure in this school we've got worse.'

But she was wrong. These were, by far, the most unhappy children in the school.

Until the angel came.

2

'Why are you all staring at me?'

Nobody thought she was an angel at first. Why should they? They were all milling about in the playground one morning before school began, when suddenly beside the high arched gates appeared a girl with a cloud of hair so gleaming bright that those who were standing near stared.

'Who's that?'

'I've never seen her before.'

'She must be new.'

And she did look new, in a way. Everything about her glowed like a freshly-minted coin. Her dress was so crisp it might have been ironed twice – inside and out. Her socks looked as if they had been pulled from the packet only a moment before. Her shoes were shop-shiny.

But she didn't look new in the other way. Most people look a bit nervous when they show up on their first morning at school, especially when it isn't even the first day of term, and they know everyone else will have had weeks and weeks, and maybe years, to find their way about and make good friends and learn the teachers' names. This newcomer didn't look in the slightest bit apprehensive. She was gazing around her as calm as you please. She looked at the stained brick walls, the peeling paint, the grimy windows and all the dustbins lined up along the wall. She read the rain-streaked sign over the door.

NITSHILL ROAD SCHOOL

Had she come all by herself?

By now, almost everyone in the playground except for Marigold had turned to look at her.

NTSHILL RD SCHOOL

She spread her hands and said in a ringing voice, clear as a bell:

'Why are you all staring at me? Am I fearfully late?'

Left to herself, Penny might have giggled. But Lisa poked her sharply in the ribs and, stepping forward, asked the girl with the shining cloud of hair:

'Have you come all by yourself?'

The newcomer gave a little shrug.

'My father was here, but he had to fly.'

Now it was Penny's turn to poke Lisa, to try and stop her giggling.

'What's your name?'

'Celeste.'

'*Celeste*?'

They didn't mean to be so rude. It just popped out.

The gold hair shimmered as Celeste tossed her head.

'It could have been worse,' she confided. 'Daddy was about to name me Angelica, but Granny swooped over just in time, and dashed the pen from his hand.'

Now people were gathering from all over the playground and standing, ears on stalks, in a ring round Celeste.

'What school do you come from?'

'I don't come from any at all. I've never been to school before.'

'What – *never*?'

'Why *not*?'

Celeste made a little face.

'I wasn't well enough. I had a million headaches, and I was so thin Granny says I could have got lost in a cucumber sandwich. My wobbly knees refused to carry me, and all the doctors said I'd never make old bones.'

She smiled seraphically.

'Then I got better. And so here I am.'

And there she was. But what to do with her? Clearly, she ought to be handed over to one of the teachers. So Penny stood on one side of her and Lisa on the other, and they started to march her, like a prisoner between guards, over the playground and right across Barry Hunter's flight path.

He saw them coming.

Penny's hand tightened round her bag of crisps. *Oh, please don't,* she thought. *Not now. Not with someone new watching.*

But already he was screeching round in one of his wide curves.

'Emergency! Emergency! The moving mountain is looming out of the mist! Swerve to avoid a crash! Boy, is she *huge*!'

Celeste stopped walking. She turned to Penny, and asked pleasantly:

'Poor boy. Is he *mental*?'

Penny couldn't even try to answer. For one thing she was forcing back hot tears of embarrassment and shame. And for another, she'd never dare say anything about Barry Hunter to someone she didn't know in case it got back to him and made him worse.

But Lisa wasn't worried.

'That's Barry Hunter,' she was telling Celeste. 'He's a big bully. He bullies everyone.'

Again, Celeste stopped to look back. Now Barry Hunter was tormenting Mark, snatching his pencil-box from him as he steered past.

'Give it back!'

'What?'

'That box. It's mine. Give it back.'

Mark stamped over the playground after Barry. But Barry was quicker on his feet. Prancing and dancing backwards as Mark advanced, he held the box a few inches from Mark's grasping fingers.

'Say please!'

'It's my box. You snatched it. Give it back!'

'Manners! Say please.'

The bell was ringing now.

'Give it back.'

Mr Fairway appeared in the doorway.

'Give it back!'

Mark was almost in tears.

'Say please,' tormented Barry.

'Please,' muttered Mark.

'A bit louder. I can't hear you.'

'*Please,*' shouted Mark in desperation.

'That's not polite,' said Barry. 'Now say it nicely.'

Mark was about to launch himself on his tormentor when suddenly Barry Hunter let out a scream of pain and swirled about, dropping the pencil-box and clutching the back of his leg.

'Who did *that*?' he yelped.

Celeste was standing right behind, eyeing him steadily.

Mr Fairway was very close now.

'What's going on over here?'

Barry knew when to cut his losses. He was about to melt away when Celeste's ringing tones stopped everyone in their tracks.

'I do believe I bit him,' she was telling the teacher.

Mr Fairway was astonished.

'*Bit* him? But *why*?'

Celeste spread her hands and said vaguely:

'Such herds of new faces. One cannot like them *all* . . .'

The bell rang once again. Mr Fairway brushed his hand through his hair.

'Now this isn't a very good start, is it, Celeste?'

Celeste turned her angelic face up towards him and said cheerfully:

'Oh, scold me if you must. But not so hard I cry, because once I start, I weep buckets.'

Mr Fairway let out a soft moan of horror. He was still standing wondering what to do when the head teacher's voice floated over from the doorway.

'Everyone in line!' Mrs Brown was shouting.

They all obeyed at once, even Barry Hunter. Lisa took Celeste's hand and led her over to stand next to Penny. Mark fetched up at the very end of the line, as usual, fiddling with his pencil-box and dropping bits and pieces all over the tarmac. But everyone else, even Marigold, stood quietly staring at Celeste.

And no one stared harder than Mr Fairway.

3

‘Comfy as a cloud . . .’

Afterwards, no one could remember quite who it was who first guessed she was a real angel. There were enough clues, of course. Tracey overheard Mrs Brown complaining that Celeste had dropped ‘out of the blue’. When Ian took the register to the school office he heard the secretary telling Miss Featherstone that the new girl had a ‘heavenly’ accent. And Mr Fairway was reported to have muttered that Celeste was having ‘a bit of trouble coming down to earth’.

Then Lisa remembered that Celeste's father hadn't walked off that first morning. Or driven. He'd *flown*!

And that reminded Penny. How had

Celeste's granny got there in time to stop her being given the wrong name?

She'd *swooped*.

The little group who chummed down Nitshill Road had a chat at the corner.

'So what did Celeste's father want to call her, anyway?'

Penny pushed the sweet she was sucking into the pouch of her cheek, out of the way.

'Angelica, she told us.'

'*Angelica*!'

Another clue!

Tracey raced back just as the bell was ringing for afternoon school. As they pushed and shoved their way back into the classroom, she whispered to everyone round her:

'Guess what Celeste means! I looked it up in our *Name Your Baby* book. Celeste means "from heaven".'

They all peeped at Celeste. Just at that moment she was gazing up out of her frizzy halo of bright hair, and telling Mr Fairway:

'No, truly, I know this chair's old enough to have a beard, and wobbles frightfully. But it's as comfy as a cloud!'

Comfy as a *cloud*? Penny sneaked a crisp out of the bag on her lap and thought about the one and only time she'd ever gone on holiday by plane. She'd flattened her face against the small plastic window, and seen beneath her a whole land of sunlit fleecy clouds, so puffy and thick you'd think you could bounce on them forever.

So had Celeste – ? Did Celeste – ?

And she wasn't the only one wondering. The whispers ran round the room.

'Comfy as a cloud!'

'That settles it! How else would anybody *know*?'

'You only have to look at her, really . . .'

Except for Marigold, they were all looking at her now. There she sat, on her little wobbly chair. Her face glowed as if it were lit from inside with a candle. Her hair shone round her smiling face. She looked like all the angels they had ever seen in books, and films and paintings.

And clearly Mr Fairway thought so too. He didn't treat her just like one of them. Oh, he may have tried his best. But he couldn't do it. It never seemed to work. Somehow it always went wrong, because of her. She wasn't like them. She was different.

Take the day she got up from her desk in the middle of spelling.

Mr Fairway's chalk skidded to a halt on the blackboard.

'Celeste?'

She waved an airy hand.

'Don't let me distract you,' she told him. 'I'm just off to water this poor plant. It's simply *gasping*.'

'Please sit down, Celeste,' Mr Fairway said. 'This is a lesson, and the plant can wait.'

Celeste sat down.

'It's your decision, of course,' she told him kindly. 'But really, without water,

that poor plant is not long for this world.'

From that moment on, no one could concentrate on a single word Mr Fairway was saying. They all kept glancing at the poor primula wilting on the windowsill. Even Mr Fairway found that time and again his eyes were drawn back to its parched and drooping leaves.

And in the end he cracked.

'Go on, then,' he told Celeste. 'Water it if you must. But be quick about it.'

She'd done it in a flash.

The next day, when he came in with the register, she was on her feet, busily buffing away at the top of her desk with a soft cloth.

'What's that peculiar smell?' he demanded.

'Marigold,' sniggered Barry Hunter, loudly. Mr Fairway pretended that he hadn't heard, but Celeste looked up anxiously.

'What on earth are you doing, Celeste?' Mr Fairway demanded.

She pushed her hair back from her face and shrugged.

'Heaven knows, I'm not a brilliant housekeeper myself,' she admitted. 'But really, the cleaning in this school is a disgrace! The litter might just as well be a carpet, the way it's all over the floors. And as for the top of this desk, well, I'm afraid that yesterday I could hardly bring myself to rest a tired elbow on it. So I'm polishing it nicely.'

Mr Fairway sat down weakly at his desk. He didn't know what to say. And next morning, when he strolled in the room and found everybody else (except for Marigold) polishing their desks as well, he was quite lost for words.

But not Celeste.

'Ah, there you are!' She beamed at him delightedly. 'We thought you were never coming! Some of us had quite given up hope.' Then, while he was still reeling from the smell of a dozen different polish sprays, she warned him confidentially: 'Today I'm going to try and coax you into letting me off arithmetic. You see, I go all of a tremble with sums. I always have. I always will. And this morning I feel weak as a leaf. So mayn't I just loll about at my desk till I feel a little bit stronger?'

'Now listen here, Celeste – ' began Mr Fairway.

Everyone waited.

But there wasn't any more. Once again, he was speechless.

Tracey nudged Penny, who was unwrapping a sweet beneath the desk.

'She *must* be a real angel,' Tracey explained. 'A normal person couldn't get away with it. They'd get sent to Mrs Brown.'

Celeste was never sent to Mrs Brown.
She *must* have been a real angel.

4
'Stuck *again*'

Whatever they did in heaven, it wasn't arithmetic. Celeste was awful at maths. Truly awful. She was even worse than Marigold, which was saying something. She was the worst in the class.

By *far*.

Mr Fairway did his best with her.

'Try it again,' he would coax. 'One more time. I'm sure you've nearly got it. You're coming along nicely.'

She'd raise her angelic face to him, her sky-blue eyes round as saucers.

'You can say to me all the pretty things you want,' she would tell him. 'But I still won't be able to do arithmetic. Who would have thought a few horrid squiggles on a page could make a poor body so unhappy? And there's no hope. Granny says baby girls come either with brains or with yellow hair – never with both.'

'That is the silliest thing I've ever heard!' Mr Fairway cried in a passion.

'There!' Celeste wailed. 'Now you're in a pet with me! Now I shall cry.'

She never did, though. Sometimes she got cross.

'No wonder I can't do it,' she'd scowl at him. 'This classroom is sheer pandemonium. No one could *think*.'

'Tracey and Yusef are managing,' Mr Fairway would point out tartly.

Celeste would sulk.

'And it's so dark in here I can barely see the book!'

Mr Fairway flicked on the light switch.

'And this pencil must be Mark's. It's chewed down to a *splinter*.'

'Celeste!' Mr Fairway said sternly. 'Stop all this complaining. Just try and get on with it, *please*. I have to go round and help other people.'

She glowered at him from under her blazing hair.

'Very well. Go round and round the class like an old *Beano*! I'll simply sit here and *rust*.'

Relieved, Mr Fairway moved away. He went up and down between the desks, helping people, till he reached Marigold, who was turning over a new page.

'Well done!' he said. 'On page 27 already! At this rate you'll soon be on to the green book!'

Marigold said something. It was so soft he couldn't hear a word. He bent his head closer, and told her:

'Say that again.'

He didn't expect that she would. But Marigold moved her head very near to his, and whispered in his ear:

'Which page is *she* on?'

He didn't need to be told which *she* Marigold wanted to know about. He

simply knew. Normally, he wouldn't answer a question like that (except, of course, to say 'You mind your own business', or 'Don't worry about anyone else. Just get on with your own work'). But Marigold had been the slowest in the class for years and years and years.

He couldn't help it. He just whispered back:

'She's halfway down page 17. And don't tell anybody, but she's stuck *again*.'

Marigold said nothing. But she gripped her pencil and lowered her head determinedly to her work-book.

Mr Fairway gave her a little look, then moved forward to the next desk.

Fancy that! he was thinking. *Who'd have believed a little thing like Celeste coming to school here would make such a change in our Marigold? Fancy that!*

5
'Fat! Fat! Fat! Fat!'

And it wasn't the only change, either. From the moment Celeste first appeared in the gateway, all sorts of things started to happen. You take the day that Barry Hunter circled Penny with his usual cry of 'Moving mountain!' and fetched up on the tarmac like a winded ten-ton starfish.

Celeste had stuck out a foot and tripped him up.

He rolled over, blood on his hands and knees. Celeste didn't wait for him to attack. She attacked first.

'My granny says you must have been born in a bucket!' she told him. 'You have no manners and you have no

brains. Now stop calling Penny fat!'

Barry Hunter thought he'd got her there.

'I didn't say "fat". *You* did.'

Celeste gave him one of her scornful looks.

'Moving mountain means *fat,*' she told him. 'Fat! Fat! Fat! Fat! But what you don't seem to realise is that if Penny stopped stuffing her face with crisps and sweeties all day long, she'd soon be as thin as I am. But you!' She pointed to him as if he were a slug on the ground. 'You're a bully! And it's harder to change that. If you're not careful, no one will ever really like you!'

Now he was scrambling to his feet, fit to kill.

'You'll be sorry!' he snarled. 'You wait!'

But Celeste had already turned away. The only thing he could have done was throw himself on her for a real fight. But she was dressed, as usual, in pure and perfect white. And she was smaller than he was. And her back was turned.

And everyone except Marigold was watching . . .

'I'll get you next break!' he yelled at her. 'You wait and see!'

'When donkeys fly!' Celeste cat-called back, and strode off with Penny. Penny was crying hard. She couldn't help it. No one had ever called her fat before. Not yelled it out like that, for everyone to hear. Oh, she knew they sometimes whispered the horrible word behind her back, out of her hearing. Even her friends did that, since it was true.

But for Celeste to shout it out like that, all over the playground!

The tears rolled down Penny's cheeks. Fat! Fat! Fat! Fat! She heard it ringing in her ears like a bell. Fat! Fat! Fat! Fat! So she couldn't understand why it was Celeste's arm she had around her shoulders. And why the grippy feeling deep inside had loosened up a bit. Was it because she knew that, next break, Barry Hunter wouldn't be bothering to run round the playground being spiteful to her? Was that it? Because she knew that, for the first time as long as she could remember, she'd probably be safe.

Barry would be after Celeste.

He tried his old trick – the one he usually played on Mark: blocking the lavatories. He'd never played it on a girl before, but they knew what was going

on the moment they saw him and his gang lined up across the entrance to the *Girls*.

Sean, Wayne, Barry himself and Stephen, who was sent round the back to block the tiny window: the whole gang.

When other girls tried to go in, the boys let them pass. Even Marigold went in without any trouble except for the usual sniffing and cries of 'What's that awful smell?' But when Celeste tried to walk past, the boys moved in quickly to push her back.

Celeste tried walking in with Lisa and Penny. All three of them were pushed back.

Lisa tried going in alone. This time, Barry Hunter and his gang didn't stop her. At the top of the steps, Lisa turned and looked back doubtfully.

'You might as well go in,' Celeste called out cheerfully. 'It's only sensible.'

So Lisa went in.

When she came out, Celeste tried

again, and she was pushed back, hard.

Then Penny tried. Again, the gang stood aside to let Penny pass. Penny, too, looked back towards Celeste, not knowing what to do.

'Go ahead,' Celeste called out. 'Before the bell rings and it's too late for you.'

So Penny went in as well.

When she appeared again, Celeste tried one last time. Sean and Wayne pushed her back, while Barry Hunter stood with his arms folded, smirking.

Shrugging, Celeste strolled away.

Barry Hunter and his gang stayed where they were, ready to block the lavatories against Celeste, right through the break. They kept an eye on her each time she ambled past, arm in arm with Lisa and Penny. She came just close enough each time to keep them on their guard. But she didn't seem bothered. And she certainly wasn't desperate. In fact, she seemed to be the most unruffled person in the playground, because everyone else was rushing from one knot of friends to the next, chattering excitedly.

Just before the bell rang, some of the other girls came near Barry Hunter's gang outside the lavatories. They giggled and pointed and stuffed their hands over their mouths. But Barry didn't realise they were laughing at him until Mr Fairway called him sharply into line, and he heard the whispers for the very first time.

'Haven't you *heard*?'

'Celeste went into the *Boys*!'

'She just walked straight in there!'

'Into the *Boys*!'

And Mr Fairway heard, too. He stared down at Celeste who was, as usual, gazing up at him with her imperturbable smile. Surely it couldn't be true! Not even Celeste . . . !

No! It must be one of those silly tales that runs round and round a school.

He took another worried peep at her.

No! Surely not even Celeste!

BOYS

6
'Normal'

While Mr Fairway was fetching the register from the office, Barry Hunter took his bad temper out on Mark.

'Shake!' he said, stopping him getting to his desk, and shoving his hand out.

Mark put his own hands safely behind his back and shook his head.

'Leave me alone,' he muttered. 'I wasn't bothering you.'

'That isn't very nice,' said Barry. 'I only want to make friends properly.'

He grinned in his lordly way at everyone who was sitting there, silently watching.

'Go on,' he told Mark again. 'Shake hands.'

Mark tried to back away between the desks. But Barry Hunter followed him.

'Shake, and I'll give you a sweetie,' he wheedled, as if he were talking to a baby. When she heard the word 'sweetie', Penny's hand slid automatically into her pocket. Then she remembered that as she was walking into Mr Hamid's shop that morning, she'd suddenly heard Celeste's pure clear voice ringing like an echo in her brain: *'If Penny stopped stuffing her face with crisps and sweeties all day long, she'd soon be as thin as I am*!' Something had made her just wave at Mr Hamid, then turn and walk out. So now she sat quietly clinking the coins that were still in her pocket, while she watched Mark going red in the face, and saying:

'I don't want a sweetie.'

He turned away. But Barry Hunter was too quick for him. Catching Mark by the arm, he forced him round and squeezed his hand so tightly that Mark yelped.

Then he gave Mark's wrist a twist-burn.

'See!' he crowed. 'I told you I'd give you a sweetie! A big barley sugar!'

The tears rolled down behind Mark's spectacles. He stumbled off blindly, just as Mr Fairway came back through the door.

'Stop clattering about, Mark!' said Mr Fairway. 'Sit *down*.'

All afternoon Barry Hunter made life difficult for poor old Mark. He tripped him up when he was called to Mr Fairway's desk. While Mark was up there, Barry took Mark's pencil-box and hid it behind the books in the corner. He dropped Mark's woolly on the floor and trod a huge footprint on it. And when Mr Fairway went out to fetch some more paper, Barry stood on his chair and announced that Mark gave walking-funny lessons every Saturday morning down at Marigold's smelly old church.

Marigold just sat there pretending she wasn't listening. But Mark took the chance of Mr Fairway being out of the room to crash about, trying to find his pencil-box.

'Sit *down*!' Mr Fairway said when he came back. 'I'm sick of telling you, Mark! Stay at your desk!'

'But – '

'No *buts*. Just sit there, *please*, and stop disturbing everyone.'

Celeste rose to her feet.

'I think you ought to know – ' she began to explain.

But Mr Fairway had had enough.

'Sit down, Celeste,' he said. 'When I want your opinion, I'll ask for it.'

Celeste sat down. All afternoon she never spoke a word. Mr Fairway smiled at her several times, trying to cajole her into answering questions he knew perfectly well she could get right. Each time she coldly turned her face away and gazed pointedly out of the window. Every few minutes she glanced at her watch, and drummed her fingers lightly on the desk top.

Mr Fairway was as glad as the rest of them when the last bell rang.

Out in the corridor, Barry Hunter pushed his way over to Celeste. You could tell from the look on his face that he was going to pay her out for trying to tell on him.

Calmly, Celeste waited till he was two feet away, then opened her mouth and screamed. Everyone stopped shoving towards the two cloakrooms and turned to stare. No one had ever heard anything like it. You'd think a police car had switched on its siren inside a biscuit tin. The noise was prodigious.

Barry Hunter backed off, fast.

As promptly as she'd turned the scream on, Celeste turned it off again.

'You'll catch it if Mrs Brown heard that,' Barry Hunter jeered.

'You'll catch it, too,' warned Celeste. 'I'll tell her all the things you did to Mark.'

Just as she said his name, Mark stumbled out of the classroom, last as usual, and tripped over one of his own feet.

Barry Hunter snorted with amusement.

'I don't know why you keep sticking up for him,' he said scornfully to Celeste. 'He's *weird*.'

Mark's face went scarlet.

'I'm not weird!'

'Well, you're not *normal*, are you?' taunted Barry. He poked Mark in the chest, and peered closely at his face through the thick bottle glasses, as if he

were looking at some insect through a microscope. 'No. You couldn't say you were *normal.*'

Suddenly Celeste was there, between the two of them.

'And you *are*, are you?' she demanded.

She turned to everyone in the corridor – not just the people from their own class, but everyone else who was shuffling into the cloakrooms.

'Who wants to be *normal*, if normal's like Barry Hunter? Barry Hunter's a bully! He's spiteful and horrid! He steals and hides things! He's a slyboots and his only real pleasure comes from making the people round him unhappy! So who wants to be *normal*?'

She gazed round.

'Come on! Speak up! Say if you want to be *normal*!'

The dead silence in the corridor spread to the cloakrooms on either side. Everyone was watching Barry Hunter and Celeste. But no one said a word.

'Right!' Celeste yelled, turning back to

him. 'Now you know, don't you! No one in this whole school wants to be normal, if being normal means being like *you*!'

Dumbstruck, the whole school watched as she slammed out.

Barry Hunter shrugged.

'She's mad,' he announced. 'She's completely off her rocker. I reckon she's even more weird than Mark the Martian. She ought to be locked up.'

One or two of them caught his eye, but nobody grinned or nodded. Nobody answered him. He was on his own. Too many of them were thinking privately how nice it would be if Barry Hunter was locked up. Or locked out. Or run over. Or *dead*. Over the years, he'd ruined so many lessons, spoiled so many games, made so many of them so unhappy. Hardly a child in the school could not remember lying in bed, dreading the day to come, thinking how wonderful school could be if people like Barry Hunter were kept in control, and they could get on with their work and enjoy their breaks – just have a normal day.

A normal school day. Wouldn't that be *weird*?

7
Round Robin

Next morning, Celeste came into school holding a big black book. Its cover was patterned with gold. Tucked down its spine was a gold pen that wrote in eight separate colours. You could choose which you wanted by twisting a fat knob.

'What's in the book, Celeste?'

'These pages are all *blank*.'

'Are you going to write in it?'

All she would tell them was:

'Wait and see.'

They didn't have to wait long. Only a few minutes later Barry Hunter came swooping round the corner, saw Marigold, and stopped to sniff.

'What's that foul smell? Is it you, Marigold?'

Marigold turned away.

He followed, sniffing ostentatiously. Then he swooped off again. When Marigold turned back, Celeste was behind her, holding the black book.

'Now what *exactly* did he say to you?'

Marigold smeared the tears across her cheek, and tried to pretend she hadn't heard.

'Come on,' Celeste ordered. 'Unbutton your beak! I have to write it down.'

Marigold stared. She stared at Celeste, then at the black book in her hand. Her eyes widened in amazement.

Then, though her eyes filled with tears when she had to repeat it, she answered Celeste's question.

'He said, "What's that foul smell? Is it you, Marigold?"'

Celeste wrote it down. Everyone crowded to watch as Celeste's golden pen moved steadily across the lines of the black book, writing the date

and time neatly in the margin, then everything that happened, down to the fact that Marigold was crying.

'You needn't put that in,' Lisa said.

Celeste ignored her. Very carefully, right at the end, she twisted the knob round from black to blue, and printed neatly:

WITNESSES:

Then she looked up.

'Who wants to be first witness?'

Nobody wanted to be first witness.

'We'll just have to do a round robin, then,' she informed them.

'What's a round robin?'

She showed them.

'Put your name here,' she ordered Mark, pointing to the bottom of the page.

Where she was pointing seemed very far away from anything she'd written. And he was dying to have a go with the fancy gold pen.

'Can I choose the colour, and twist the knob myself?'

'Yes.'

Mark couldn't resist. He had to fiddle the knob round four times before he managed to stop on the right colour. But then, triumphantly, he scratched his name in glorious fern green.

She took the pen out of his hand, and gave it to Lisa.

'And you sign your name here.'

The spot she chose was right on the edge, miles away from the writing. And Lisa longed to write her name in silver.

'Penny.'

Way over the other side, where

Celeste was pointing, Penny chose to write her name in gold. As she was doing it, she wondered how much the pen had cost. She'd saved quite a bit of money already, not buying any more crisps or sweets.

'Paul.'

He didn't hesitate.

'I'm first to use the red!'

Everyone was queuing now, keen to have a go at twisting the knob of the fancy gold pen to choose the colour for their name.

'Tracey.'

'Yusef.'

'Kelly.'

She called out names till there was hardly anybody left. Then:

'Marigold.'

Marigold shook her head.

'Go on,' everyone urged her.

She shook her head again.

'Why not?'

'We've all written our names.'

'Come on, Marigold.'

'Are you scared?'

She didn't look scared. But then again, as usual she didn't really look anything. And she didn't say anything, either. She simply stared down at the ground at her feet, and shook her head again.

Celeste turned to look for someone else.

'Wayne.'

'*Me*?'

He was only hanging about on the edge out of sheer nosiness. Usually he was part of Barry Hunter's gang. But that didn't seem to bother Celeste.

'Did you hear what he said, or didn't you?'

'Well, yes – '

'Then sign.'

Wayne hesitated. He didn't know what she was going to do with what she'd written and everyone had signed. And Barry Hunter would kill him. But, on the other hand, he really wanted to write his name in the purple.

And one more name couldn't matter.

'Where shall I put it?'

Celeste handed him the book. It was quite obvious where he should write his name. Once his was done, under Celeste's report would be a perfect ring of brightly-coloured names – no first, no last; just a circle of witnesses with no leader, no head of the gang.

Wayne signed.

'There,' said Celeste. 'That's a round robin.'

They all stared at it gravely. Then the bell rang. While they were trooping into class, Penny asked Marigold:

'Why wouldn't you write in Celeste's book?'

She never expected Marigold to answer. More often than not, if you asked Marigold a question, she just pretended that she hadn't heard.

Not this time, though. For the first time ever, Marigold looked Penny straight in the eye.

'It's wrong,' she said. 'You shouldn't

have written your name, either. Nobody should. Only the angel can write in the Book of Deeds.'

Marigold walked off, leaving Penny gaping.

Book of Deeds? What on earth?

She glanced uneasily towards Celeste.

Of course, with an angel, the question might not be 'What on earth?' at all.

It might be 'What in heaven?'

8
The Book of Deeds

Everyone sat in a circle round Marigold.

'Tell us again,' Kelly told her.

Marigold wriggled on the step.

'I've *told* you,' she said. 'I've told you everything I know a dozen times.'

'Tell us again.'

Marigold took a deep breath and told them again. Each time she told the story she added on a little bit she'd never said before. This was partly because the story seemed to grow inside her each time they made her tell it, and partly because she wanted to keep them interested. It was quite nice to sit up on the step with everyone gathered round, listening hard. It kept her safe from

Barry Hunter. And it was a bit like having lots of friends.

She told them all over again.

'I heard about it in church. There is an angel who is beautiful and perfect and stands at heaven's gate – '

'Like she stood at ours.'

All eyes swivelled to the gates through which, at any moment, they expected her.

'And this angel has a name, the Recording Angel, because his job – '

'*Her* job – '

'The angel's job is to write everything you ever did in your whole life – whether it's good or bad – down neatly in the Book of Deeds.'

Last time she'd added 'neatly'. This time she embroidered the story a little bit more.

'If it was a good deed, the angel smiles writing it down.'

'She smiles a lot.'

'And if it's a bad deed, the angel weeps.'

There was a slightly embarrassed pause. No one liked to mention that Celeste never wept. Oh, they couldn't count the number of times she'd said to Mr Fairway: 'Don't make me finish my sums. It isn't worth it. I'll just sit and *howl.*' But, so far, no one had ever seen a single tear in her eye.

Marigold knew what they were thinking, but she pressed on anyway.

'But even the angel's tears can't wash out what is written down. Whatever the deed was, it stays in the book for ever and ever.'

There was the usual grave silence. Ian held out his crisp bag and everyone except Penny dipped in to take one while they had a think. Then Kelly said:

'He's going to be in such trouble when he gets to heaven's gate. She's used up half the book already, writing down the horrid things he does.'

'She never makes anything up, though.' Yusef defended Celeste.

'The truth, the whole truth, and nothing but the truth,' said Elaine.

Their eyes searched out Barry Hunter. He was over the other side of the playground, all alone, kicking a box to bits. Over the last weeks, his gang had dwindled to almost no one. Wayne never even tried to make friends again, after being a witness in Celeste's book. He just went off with Stephen, who was pretty fed up with always being the one sent round the back to guard the window when they blocked the lavatories. That only left Sean. And Sean was often off school.

So Barry Hunter spent more and more of his time mucking about by himself. He was still bullying, but it wasn't the same now that each time he tried it a dozen people came running from far and wide to watch him do his worst, all shouting eagerly:

'Bags be first witness!'

'No! Let *me*!'

There was still plenty for the Book of Deeds, though. When Celeste opened it on any page, everyone would peer over her shoulder to read it.

Thursday, 4 May

8.46 Barry Hunter wouldn't stop putting his head under Mark's toilet door when he needed to be private. He said it was 'only a joke'.

Witnesses: Ian. Wayne. Yusef. Mark.

8.56 Barry Hunter kept bumping into people on the way to Assembly. He said 'Stop bumping' loudly to everyone he bumped, but it was really him bumping. Paul, Nessa and Zabeen say he wasn't bumping hard, he was just annoying. Wayne says his bump really hurt (and he had to bump back a bit).

Witnesses: Wayne. Zabeen. Nessa. Celeste. Kelly. Ian. Lisa. Penny. Phil. Paul. Mark. Elaine. Yusef. (And Mr Fairway gave Barry one of his looks, so he must have seen too.)

9.50 Barry Hunter sniffed near Marigold and said, 'What's that horrible smell?' twice.

9.51 He did it again.
9.53 And again.
Witnesses: Lisa. Penny. Ian. Phil. Nessa. (We didn't ask Marigold because she was upset, and she doesn't sign anyway.)
10.30 Barry Hunter ruined Claire and Elaine's Fashion Show. First he hid some of the clothes behind the pipes, so there wasn't much time left. Then, when the people in the show were taking their turns to show their fashions off, he started booing loudly. So everyone in the show got embarrassed and wouldn't do it properly. So Mr Fairway stopped the show. (Barry Hunter wasn't the *only* one to boo, but he was *definitely* the one who started it.)
Witnesses: Claire. Elaine. Phil. Ian. Zabeen. Tracey. P.T.O.

And all that was just on one page. No wonder everyone crowded round

Marigold, keen to hear any tiny thing she could remember about what happened with a Book of Deeds. No wonder, when Celeste finally sailed through the gates, her gleaming frock mirroring the shine of her hair, her eyes bright with excitement, everyone (even Marigold) ran over to greet her.

'Where have you *been*?'

Celeste spread her hands.

'Disaster! Last night I cried so much I had to peg up my pillowcase. I'm being moved.'

'Moved?'

Everyone was horrified.

'Moved *where*?'

'Moved *how*?'

'*Why*?'

Celeste settled on the step, and tucked her frock neatly around her.

'Blame my father entirely!' she told them. 'Granny has told him time and again that trying to teach me arithmetic is like trying to plough the sea. But he won't rest. First he harped on about it, day and night. Now it seems he's been flitting from school to school, green with worry, looking for somewhere a dilly like me can learn to slap eight and eight together, and make fourteen.'

'Sixteen,' they corrected her, but she wasn't listening. She was far too excited.

'And so I'm to be swept off again, like a loose leaf tumbling around the world.'

'But where?'

'When?'

She made a face.

'Almost at once. Would you believe, I've even had to beg for these few hours to totter in and exchange a few sad farewells!'

In the shocked silence that followed, the ringing of the bell came almost as a relief.

Celeste rose to her feet, sighing, and brushed an invisible speck from her frock.

'Come along,' she told them. 'Let's go and break the news. I shall sob so hard

Mr Fairway will have to mop all the floors behind me as I go.'

Appalled, they set off in a bunch across the playground. Her eyes still shining, she strolled after them.

9

'Only a joke. Only a game.'

Before they reached the school door, they heard Barry Hunter shouting.

'Bombs away!'

Everyone spun round to watch as Barry swung back his foot and, giving the old box one last tremendous boot, sent it flying – up, up, up and over.

It landed – plop! – on top of poor Mark's head.

'Bull's eye!' yelled Barry Hunter.

They all stood waiting for Mark to tear the box off his head. They were waiting for the red face. They were waiting for the tears and the temper. Tracey said, 'Bags be first witness,' and everyone else looked round to check that

Celeste was carrying her big black book and her fancy gold pen.

Mark staggered round the playground like a robot out of control.

Above Penny's head, the staff-room window opened, and she heard Mrs Brown ask Mr Fairway anxiously:

'Is he *hurt*?'

Like everyone in the playground, Mr Fairway watched Mark swivel his head round as if he were looking for radio signals.

'No,' Penny heard him say. 'I think he's actually making a bit of a joke of it.'

Mrs Brown sounded astonished.

'Mark? Making a joke of something Barry Hunter did to him? Now there's a change!'

Just at that moment, Marigold ran up to offer Mark a guiding hand.

'Am I *dreaming*?' said Mrs Brown. 'Is that *Marigold* who just ran up and joined in the game?'

'She was telling them all Bible stories yesterday,' said Miss Featherstone.

'I don't believe it!' Mrs Brown said. Then, glancing down, she noticed Penny just beneath the window. Quickly, Penny ran off, pretending she was going to help Marigold steer Mark away from all the people standing round clapping his brilliant robot act. The last thing she overheard was Mrs Brown saying:

'Really, that child Penny's clothes are practically falling off her! It's time she

tightened her buttons.'

For the twentieth time that day, Penny hitched her skirt up and grinned. She wasn't going to tighten her buttons. Not yet! Having your clothes flapping was much nicer than having them bulging.

Now Marigold had lifted the battered old box off Mark's head. The joke was over, so Penny joined the gang of people crowding round Celeste.

'Can I be first and sign in the silver?'

'Let me be yellow!'

'Bags be green!'

But Celeste hadn't even opened the black book.

'There's nothing to write,' she told them. 'Everyone had a good time. If someone's unhappy, then it goes in the book. If everyone's happy, then it doesn't.'

They all thought about it for a moment. It seemed fair enough, as rules went. Much fairer, anyway, than letting Barry Hunter get away with making people miserable and then saying: 'Only a joke. Only a game.'

Yes. It was a good way to judge.

Content, they watched Celeste tuck the black book safely away under her arm. Content, they followed her into the school.

10
Goodbye, Celeste

'The bell hasn't rung yet,' said Mrs Brown. 'Why is everyone in your class except Barry Hunter inside?'

Mr Fairway sighed and put his mug down on the draining board.

'Blame Celeste,' he said. 'Since she came, none of them have been the same.'

Mrs Brown glanced at him thoughtfully.

'Perhaps that's no bad thing,' she said. 'When you remember how some of them were before.'

He thought about that all down the corridor. It was so much on his mind that when the school secretary popped her head round the office door and said, 'Guess who's leaving?' he answered right first time.

'Celeste!'

So *that* was why the whole lot had trooped in before the bell. To bring him the sad news. And he *was* sad. She was a strange little creature, but he would miss her.

He pushed the classroom door open.

There they all stood in a half circle around her. Celeste had even more of a glow than usual on her face. In fact, she looked radiant.

'Well!' he said, sitting heavily at his desk. 'This is a sad day.'

She gave him one of her celestial smiles.

'I have something for you,' she told him, and nodded to Marigold, who stepped up and gave him a black book patterned with gold. At first, from the solemn way she handed it over, he thought that it must be a Bible. But then he realised it was the book he'd seen them poring over so often in the playground. And in the cloakrooms. And in class.

'Thank you,' he said, and opened it to take a look inside.

It was a shock. A horrid, horrid book. An ugly catalogue of pain and humiliation and fear and spite. He felt sick reading it. He turned over two or three more pages, feeling all their eyes on him, then raised his own to Celeste.

'Is this really what you're leaving me?' he asked. 'A book of tale-telling.'

Celeste said steadily:

'Granny says the rule not to tell tales was invented by bullies – ' Her sky-blue eyes met his across the desk. 'And the people who don't really want to stand up to them.'

He couldn't meet her gaze any longer. He looked down. Another horrid passage caught his eye. He read it to the end. Oh, poor, poor Marigold! No wonder she went round pretending to be deaf, if that's what she heard all day! And Mark! The number of times he must have been tricked into getting into trouble. And Penny! 'Moving mountain' indeed! And all the other things that happened to the rest. How horrible to be kept from using the lavatory, or fetching your coat! How nasty to have your things snatched and hidden all day long! Your games ruined, your family called rude names, your jacket torn and muddied.

'Why didn't anyone tell me all this was going on?'

Those sky-blue eyes again. She didn't answer. She knew as well as he did, as well as they all did, that he'd known everything he needed all along. But just like Marigold he had pretended not to see, not to hear, not to understand.

He slammed the book shut so hard it made them jump.

'Right!' he said. 'I've read enough!'

This time he managed to meet her eye. He really meant what he said.

'Things will be very different around here from now on.'

'You promise to keep the book?'

'Here in my desk,' he promised her. 'As long as I'm teaching in this school.'

'Just to remind you . . .'

'To remind me.'

Again, their eyes met. She was satisfied. Smiling, she stuck out her hand.

'Well, then. Goodbye,' she said, as if she were leaving a party. 'Thank you very much for having me. I hope I haven't been too much trouble.'

Mr Fairway came round the desk. Blinking his tears away, he gave her a giant hug.

'Trouble?' he said. 'Nonsense! Listen, Celeste. Wherever you go, I want you to tell them that we thought you were a real *angel*. And in the few weeks we were lucky enough to have you at Nitshill Road School, you have worked *wonders*.'

She hugged him back. Then she

hugged everyone else. Then she was off. On her way to the door, she dropped the gold pen on to Barry Hunter's desk, and turned to wink at them.

And even those who were astonished winked back.

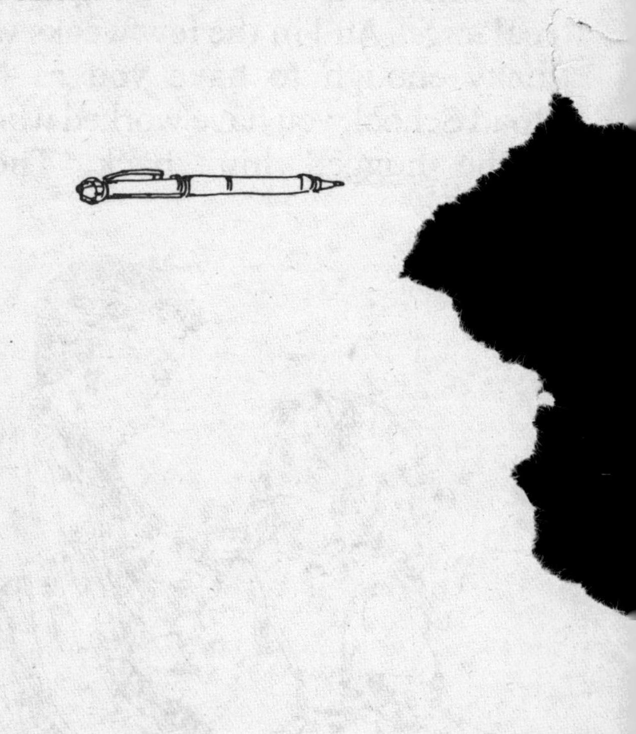